"Is there something you're not telling me?" Chris asked.

It would have been easy to tell Chris her secret right now. Just a few little words. *I have lupus.* But she couldn't say it. Not now. It was too nice to feel like a normal girl falling in love, not someone who'd need to be rushed to the hospital at any moment. If Chris found out how sick she was, it was bound to change the way he looked at her. Chris, she was sure, wanted a girlfriend he could have fun with, go places with, look forward to the future with. Not a girl who had no future.

"It's nothing," Holly said, smiling at him. "I was just thinking how happy I am to be with you, and how I wish this moment never had to end."

"It doesn't have to, Holly." Holly felt absolutely weightless as Chris gathered her in his arms and let his lips touch hers.

Also in the Point Romance series:

Look out for:

Last Summer, First Love:
Goodbye to Love
Jennifer Baker

Summer Sizzlers
Various

Two-Timer
Lorna Read

Russian Nights
Robyn Turner

Point Romance

LAST SUMMER, FIRST LOVE

A Time to Love

Created by
JENNIFER BAKER

Written by
CARIN GREENBERG BAKER

SCHOLASTIC

Scholastic Children's Books,
Scholastic Publications Ltd,
7-9 Pratt Street, London NW1 OAE, UK

Scholastic Inc.,
555 Broadway, New York, NY 10012-3999, USA

Scholastic Canada Ltd,
123 Newkirk Road, Richmond Hill,
Ontario, Canada L4C 3G5

Ashton Scholastic Pty Ltd,
PO Box 579, Gosford, New South Wales,
Australia

Ashton Scholastic Ltd,
Private Bag 94407, Greenmount, Auckland,
New Zealand

First published in the US by Scholastic Inc, 1994
First published in the UK by Scholastic Publications Ltd, 1995

ISBN 0 590 55858 7

Printed by Cox & Wyman Ltd, Reading, Berks.

Chapter One

"I'm going to miss you so much," Holly Paige said, wrapping her arms around her best friend, Sarah Badler. "I wish you didn't have to go."

Sarah hugged Holly back hard. "It's just for the summer," she said cheerfully, though her dark brown eyes shone with tears. "Before you know it, I'll be right back here in my usual booth, ordering my usual breakfast."

"Two eggs over easy, English muffin, hash browns," Holly said, laughing through her own tears. "But maybe after you've braved the rapids of Colorado, you won't *want* to come home to boring old Landon."

Sarah had been one of Holly's two best friends since second grade. Now, after senior year of high school—well, Sarah's anyway—

Sarah was heading out west to lead white-water rafting trips on the Colorado River. Holly had never been farther west than Burlington, Vermont, which was practically a major metropolis compared to tiny Landon. She'd never even been out of the state.

Not that she didn't want to. Holly had once dreamed of going a lot farther than Colorado. Like China, maybe, or Africa or India. The farther away and the more exotic, the better. Holly had always been fascinated with how different groups of people lived all over the world. She'd fantasized about becoming an explorer or an anthropologist or a photojournalist.

Now it looked as if she'd never get much farther than the four walls of Peg's, her mother's diner, where she worked as a waitress. Holly sighed and stared at the chipped Formica tables with their worn red vinyl booths, the counter that ran the length of the long, narrow restaurant, the ancient jukebox that still played 45's.

The only thing older than the jukebox was Mr. Deerfield, who sat at the next booth drinking black coffee and eating a cherry Danish. Mr. Deerfield had been the town barber since 1927 and had only retired a few years ago when his hands got too shaky to hold the scissors.

"You guys aren't getting all weepy on me again, are you?" asked Holly's other best friend, Erica Granville, returning from the jukebox.

Erica's hair color this week was platinum blond with a single streak of pink to match a new pair of pink cowboy boots she'd bought for *her* big summer trip. Erica's parents were divorced, and Erica always spent July and August with her dad in San Francisco.

"It's only two months," Erica said stubbornly, slipping into the booth across from Holly and Sarah. "We'll all be back together again, just like always."

"Right," Sarah agreed, sniffling. "Two months. That's practically no time at all."

Or all the time I have left, Holly couldn't help thinking. For the past year she'd tried her best to be optimistic, but there was no way to avoid the truth. Holly was sick with lupus or, to be absolutely accurate, *systemic lupus erythematosus.* It had started a few years ago with a weird, scaly red rash on her nose and cheeks that got worse whenever she went in the sun. The rash came and went, and Dr. Frazier hadn't seemed too worried. Lots of people had lupus, especially women, and most of them lived perfectly normal lives.

But a year ago, the disease had taken a turn for the worse. Holly had started getting fevers and feeling weak and tired all the time, so weak she couldn't get out of bed. Her knees had swelled up so much, she couldn't have walked even if she'd had the energy. It had gotten so bad, she'd had to spend half the year in the hospital and the other half in her own bed. She'd missed everything—her senior year of high school, the prom, and graduating with her friends.

The only bright spot in all this was that this past spring she'd started to feel a whole lot better. The fever and swelling and tiredness had disappeared, and she almost felt like her old self.

Holly had learned too much about lupus to be hopeful, though. The illness could come back at any time—and could get a lot worse. She could have seizures. She could go blind. Or she could get kidney damage so bad that she could die. There was nothing she or any of the doctors could do to stop it. All she could do was try to take care of herself—to rest, stay out of the sun, and avoid stress. So much for seeing the world. There was a chance she might not even be around when Sarah and Erica got back from their summer vacations.

But I'm not gonna think like that, Holly told herself fiercely. *There's also a chance I'll be around for a good long time. And as long as that's a possibility, that's what I'm going to focus on.*

"Two months will go by just like that," Holly said, snapping her fingers and grinning. "I mean, there's so much happening in town this summer that I don't know how I'll be able to keep up with it all. Harry's Homemade Ice Cream Parlor has three new flavors *and* two new video games."

Glancing over at ninety-eight-year-old Mr. Deerfield, who was noisily sipping his coffee, Holly lowered her voice. "And I heard a rumor that this may be the summer when Mr. Deerfield finally hands over his car keys to the town deputy." Mr. Deerfield's vision wasn't what it used to be, and he'd had a couple of collisions with the maple tree at the end of Main Street. It was a good thing he never drove more than five miles an hour.

Sarah laughed and playfully slapped Holly's shoulder. "You're impossible."

"And don't change," Erica added. "I'm really gonna miss your sense of humor."

The front door jingled and a lanky man with a beard and mustache ambled in and headed for the counter. He was in his mid-thirties and wore a rumpled T-shirt and faded jeans. If Holly hadn't known who he was, she would have thought he worked at one of the local dairy farms or maybe the lumber mill right outside of town. In fact, he was Jay Lawrence, multimillionaire president of The New England Mountain Bike Company. Practically half the town of Landon worked for him—the half that didn't work at The Mountain, the mega-glitzy resort nearby.

But you'd never know it just by looking at him. Jay Lawrence ate breakfast at Peg's Diner every day, lived in a small red-shingled house right on Main Street, and sent his kids to Landon's public schools even though most of Landon's rich sent their kids away to boarding school. Jay (he wouldn't let anybody call him Mr. Lawrence) was always talking about how much he loved Landon's small-town values. Holly tried not to laugh whenever she heard this. Jay had been born and raised in New York City. If he'd been born here, he'd be trying to get *out* like everyone else she knew.

Jay took a seat at the counter and picked up a plastic-coated menu.

"I'd better get back to work," Holly said, standing up and smoothing her wrinkled apron.

"I've got to finish packing anyway," Sarah said. She reached into her pocket and pulled out her wallet.

"Oh, no you don't," Holly said. "This one's on us. You guys have a great summer."

Sarah and Erica got out of the booth and hugged Holly at the same time.

"A Holly Sandwich," Erica said, laughing. "You should put that on the menu."

The musical intro to an old song came over the jukebox speaker. "Perfect timing!" Erica said, launching into the lyrics of "See You in September." Erica's version, however, was purposely loud and off-key.

"Please!" Holly begged, covering her ears. "Get out before you crack the glasses!"

Sarah gave Holly a peck on the cheek. "I'll send you postcards," she said. "And I promise to call."

"Me, too," Erica said as she and Sarah walked toward the front door. "And you know my number."

Sarah and Erica lingered at the door, shooting Holly such sorrowful looks that Holly couldn't stand it anymore. If she was going to have any hope at all of surviving, she needed a little help.

"Bye!" Holly said brightly, opening the door for them. "I'll be here when you get back. I promise."

Three preppy teenaged boys pushed past Holly and headed for a booth. Tall and tan, they wore tennis whites and talked and laughed loudly, drowning out the quiet chatter of the diner. Holly had never seen them before, but she could guess exactly who they were and where they came from: guests of The Mountain, who showed up during ski season or in the summer, but always acted like they owned the town.

Rolling her eyes, Holly pulled out her order pad and headed for Jay at the counter. "Cheddar cheese omelette, side of sausage, small orange juice?" she asked, uncapping her pen.

Jay pulled thoughtfully at his beard. "Hmmm . . ." he said. "Maybe I'll be different just for once."

Holly's pen paused just above the pad. This was a first. Like most of her customers, Jay always ordered the same thing every day.

"Make that a *large* orange juice," Jay said.

Holly smiled. "Coming right up." She quickly jotted down Jay's order.

"How are you feeling?" Jay asked with concern.

"Much better, thanks," Holly said. "I'm in remission."

Jay smiled broadly. "That's great!"

"Thank you again for all you did," Holly said. "You were unbelievably generous." Holly's parents had gone into debt, tens of thousands of dollars, to pay her medical bills. But the whole town had chipped in to help pay for some of it. There'd been bake sales, tag sales, even collection cups in all the local stores and restaurants. Jay Lawrence, alone, had chipped in five thousand dollars.

"I didn't do anything," Jay insisted. "I'm just glad you're feeling better."

Holly turned and clipped Jay's breakfast order to the window that led to the kitchen.

"Wait a second, Holly," Jay said. "How come you haven't entered my contest?"

"What contest?"

Jay smiled. "Don't tell me you haven't seen the flyers I've put up all over town. I've come up with a great new advertising campaign for my company. I intend to pick a local girl or guy who best represents the wonderful small-town values of Landon and have them model with my bikes. I'm calling it The Spirit of the Mountains."

"Sounds good," Holly said. "I guess I just didn't see the flyers."

"You'd be perfect for my ad," Jay said. "You've got that New England wholesomeness I'm looking for. What do you say? Are you interested in entering? Winner gets a free mountain bike."

The Spirit of the Mountains. Holly shivered. This was hitting a little too close to home. If she didn't beat her illness, a spirit was all she'd be, a ghostly presence still floating around this tiny town, stuck here for eternity. She also had a feeling Jay was encouraging her to enter only because he felt sorry for her. She appreciated his generosity, but she didn't want the whole town to think of her as a charity case anymore.

"I'm very flattered," Holly said, "but modeling's not my thing. I'm sure there're lots of other people who'd be interested, though."

"Excuse me," said a girl's voice from down the counter. "I hope I'm not disturbing you, but *I'd* be interested."

Holly looked toward the voice and had to sti-

fle a laugh when she recognized the slender girl
with the perfect strawberry-blond curls. Cynthia
Dansby? The Spirit of the Mountains? Holly had
known Cynthia since kindergarten, and she was
sure Cynthia had never gone near a mountain,
a lake, or anything remotely natural. Cynthia
probably wouldn't even have gone outside if
she'd had a choice. Cynthia's clothes were
always perfectly pressed, her nails were always
polished—never chipped—and she'd never had
a run in her stocking. In fact, Cynthia was the
only girl Holly knew who even *wore* stockings.

Jay smiled politely at Cynthia. "You can
drop off a photo of yourself at our office. The
deadline's five o'clock today. We'll be selecting
our finalists tonight."

"Thank you," Cynthia said, rising from her
stool. "Of course, I'm not as *natural* as Holly,
but then again, I don't think it's a bad idea for
a girl to fix herself a little bit, do you? A little
blush does wonders for a pale complexion."
With a snide little smile at Holly, Cynthia
grabbed her bill off the counter and headed
for the cash register.

Holly barely squashed the impulse to stick
out her tongue at Cynthia. So what if she was
pale? She wasn't allowed to go in the sun. And

it was none of Cynthia's business if she didn't choose to wear makeup.

Holly was mad at herself for even letting Cynthia get to her. Still, she couldn't help glancing at her reflection in the top of the toaster on the counter beneath the kitchen window. Her skin was very white, in sharp contrast to her dark, straight hair. She'd gained back some of the weight she'd lost in the hospital, but her high cheekbones stood out sharply against her thin face. Her dark eyes were framed by thick black lashes, and her mouth was wide and full. All in all, not too bad for an invalid.

But what difference did it make what she looked like? She hadn't even had a date in the past year, and with her future so uncertain, there was no point even *looking* for romance. No. True, everlasting love was definitely out of the question.

"Hey you! Waitress!" one of the tennis preppies sang out, snapping his fingers in the air. "We'd like to order one of these years."

Holly took her time getting to their booth. She hadn't purposely kept the preppies waiting, but if they were going to be so rude, they could wait a little longer. "Yes?" Holly asked when she reached the table.

"What do you recommend?" asked the guy

who'd been snapping his fingers so impatiently. He had chiseled features, glossy black hair, and he was wearing a Dover Prep T-shirt.

"Oh," Holly said sweetly. "Do you need help reading the menu?"

The guy's face turned red and his blond friend sitting next to him laughed. "Touché!" he said, smiling up at Holly. There was something vaguely familiar about him, though Holly couldn't figure out why. As she stared at him a moment, he looked back at her with equal intensity like he, too, was trying to remember something.

"Someone's got to teach Brett some manners," the blond guy said to Holly, "and I bet you're just the girl to do it." There was something familiar about the way he spoke, too. And his smile. For some reason, Holly could picture those even white teeth behind braces. And instead of that lean face, Holly saw chubby cheeks.

"Well, ordinarily I love a challenge," Holly said, "but I think I'm busy for the next few years."

"Too bad," the blond guy said, "'cause I might have some free time. I thought you might be able to give me some private lessons when you're done with Brett."

This guy was cute, and he was clearly flirting with her, but Holly had seen preppies in action too many times to take any of them seriously. She knew how their minds worked. Townie waitresses were fine for a date, even a quickie summer fling, but these Bretts and Bradleys and Bradford III's always ended up with preppie girls their parents had picked out for them.

"Are we ever ordering or what?" demanded the guy on the other side of the table. He had round, wire-rimmed glasses and his light brown hair was slicked straight back off his high forehead.

"Yeah, Chris," Brett complained. "I'm starving!"

Chris? Why wasn't Holly the least bit surprised to hear that was the blond guy's name? Chris . . . Christopher . . . Chubby cheeks, braces, freckles, a blond brush cut . . . it was all coming back to Holly now. At the same moment, Chris gave her a sharp look.

"Holly Paige?" he asked.

Holly nodded, and a chill went down her spine. "Christopher Franklin?"

Then they both spoke at the same time. "Oh, no!"

Chapter Two

June Paige, Holly's fifteen-year-old sister, pushed away her half-eaten bowl of soggy cereal and jumped up from the kitchen table. She was too excited to eat. Today was the first day of her summer job at The Mountain Resort, the job that was going to change her life forever. Grabbing her bowl, June raced for the kitchen sink.

"Hold it!" her father said from his seat at the head of the large wooden table that nearly filled the tiny kitchen. "You're not finished."

"I'm not hungry," June insisted, quickly dumping her cereal into the garbage disposal. "And I've got to go. I don't want to be late."

Tom Paige's jowled face fell into a frown. "I don't know why you're in such a hurry to work for the Franklins after what they did to this town," he said. "Landon used to be quiet and peaceful before they started bringing in all those out-of-towners. It's like the town doesn't belong to us anymore."

June sighed as she looked at her father's tired face. His salt-and-pepper hair was getting whiter every day and his once trim body was going soft in the middle. Her father hadn't been the same ever since the Franklins built The Mountain Resort ten years ago.

Tom Paige had once been mayor of Landon—a part-time, non-paying job, of course, since the town had only had 563 people. But he'd loved being in charge of the tiny town where his family had lived for the past five generations. Then the Franklins had moved here and bought up hundreds of acres so they could build the biggest ski and summer resort in the state.

June's father had fought the resort as long as he could. He'd tried to rally Landon against the Franklins, but he couldn't compete with their money, power, and all the jobs they were offering. He'd not only lost the battle, but he'd even lost the house his family had lived in for the past 120 years. Once The Mountain had been built and all the tourists started coming, taxes went so high that Tom Paige couldn't afford to keep his house anymore.

But unlike her father, June wasn't bitter. "I like it better now," she insisted. "The Mountain's brought a little life to this hole-in-the-wall place."

"You mean it's brought *boys*," said June's younger sister, Annie. She giggled and slurped orange juice through a Krazy Straw.

"Yeah, agreed Annie's identical twin, Sally, noisily crunching on a piece of whole-wheat toast and sending crumbs flying all over the table. "That's all she ever talks about."

Annie and Sal were eleven years old and would be starting junior high school in the fall. They were short, wiry, and athletic, with full heads of thick, dark hair. June had loved taking care of them when they were smaller, but now they were getting far too nosy and far too interested in her love life.

"Did you see that guy June was hanging out with last week at Harry's Homemade Ice Cream Parlor?" Annie gossiped.

"The one with the long hair and the earring?" Sal asked.

"What guy?" their father demanded, glancing sternly at June.

"Oh, no one," June said, glaring at her younger sisters. "Just a guy from school." Actually, that guy *was* no one. Just some local kid who'd graduated from high school and was starting a job on the loading docks at The New England Mountain Bike Company. He was nobody June would ever be interested in.

"I've got to get ready for work," June said, loading her bowl into the dishwasher and racing from the kitchen.

"June!" her father called after her. "We're still not finished talking about that job."

June sighed as she hurried up the stairs to her room. It seemed her job at The Mountain was all she and her father *ever* talked about. Her father didn't approve, that was clear. But he hadn't absolutely forbidden her to work there. Even if he had, June would have found some way to do it. It was all part of her master plan.

June entered the small bedroom she shared with Holly and grabbed her knapsack off the hook behind the door. Then she raced to the double dresser that filled the space between the twin beds. She needed just the right outfit for her first day on the job. Yanking open the bottom right drawer, June fished around until she found the tiny black string bikini.

"*That's* what you're wearing to work?" Annie asked, giggling at the door.

"I thought the help wasn't allowed to use the pool," Sal piped in, peering around from behind Annie. She still had toast crumbs on her chin.

"You guys mind your own business," June snapped, dropping the bikini in her knapsack. Crossing the few steps it took to reach the door, June closed it and locked it, but she could still hear her sisters giggling outside.

Of course, they were absolutely right. June would be working as a maid this summer, and The Mountain staff wasn't allowed to use guest facilities. June had been told that loud and clear at her job interview. But that had all been factored into her plan.

Opening her closet door, June reached up onto a high shelf and pulled down a small plastic bag. In it was a wig, its coppery red, straight hair cut shoulder length with bangs. June slipped it on and looked at her reflection in the mirror. Then she found her sunglasses on the dresser top and put those on, too. She grinned at her reflection. Sure, the round face and full lips were still the same, but no one really knew her at The Mountain. If they saw her at the pool, they'd never recognize her as the girl who cleaned their rooms.

Of course, it was breaking the rules, but how else was she going to meet one of those cute, rich boys who drove up and down Main Street in their BMW's and Mercedes convertibles? How else was she going to find someone to take her away from this tiny little house and the cramped room she shared with her sister, the shabby diner with its smells of grease and ketchup and coffee grounds?

The Paige family hadn't always lived this way. June crossed to the window over Holly's bed and looked out past the fields, up the hill to an old, white colonial farmhouse. The large, rambling house had Vermont green shutters and wraparound porches. A little ways above the house, in a clearing in the woods behind it, was a small round gazebo overlooking all of Landon.

That was the house June's family used to live in until the taxes got too high and they couldn't afford it anymore. June had had her own room then, in the attic with a huge stone fireplace and a window seat. Their kitchen alone had been as large as the whole bottom floor of the little house they lived in now. And they'd had thirty acres of woods and fields to roam around in.

All her father had been able to hold on to was a half acre at the edge of their old property. And their old house was only occupied now during ski season by some rich family from Connecticut. It was such a waste, and so unfair. But June wasn't going to get all depressed about it the way her father did. She'd decided she was going to *do* something about it. She was going to live again the way they had in their old house. Maybe even better. She was going to have money and houses and cars and all the things those rich tourists had. She'd be so rich she could buy a cure for Holly's lupus. Price would be no object. That was when she'd formed her plan to work at The Mountain.

"June!" her father called, banging on the door.

Uh-oh. June didn't want to get trapped into another pointless conversation when her mind was so firmly made up. She glanced at the window, wondering if there was any way she could escape through there, but she didn't want to break her neck falling out a second-story window. And even if she got out in one piece, she'd still have to face her father when she got home.

"What?" June asked patiently, unlocking and opening the door.

"It's almost eight-thirty," her father said,

holding out his grandfather's gold pocket watch, which was attached to the belt loop of his faded jeans. "If you insist on working as hired help to the Franklins, at least show them who raised you. A Paige is never late and a Paige always lives up to his responsibility."

"Or *her* responsibility," June joked, "since four out of five of us are female."

"Right," her father said. "And when you get tired of making the Franklins' beds and emptying their garbage, your mother could use a hand at the diner."

June sighed. Her father was never going to quit harping on this subject. And what was the difference between cleaning up after guests at the hotel and wiping dirty counters at Peg's? But she didn't have time for another argument, and at least her father wasn't going to stand in her way.

"Gotta go," she said, giving him a quick peck on the cheek. Grabbing her knapsack, she raced down the stairs and out the front door before her father could change his mind.

Chapter Three

"You two *know* each other?" Brett asked Holly and Chris back at the diner. His tone clearly indicated surprise that the rich, handsome son of the owner of The Mountain even knew the name of a lowly local like her.

"*Knew* is more like it," Chris said. "Landon Elementary School."

"We were in the same class in sixth grade," Holly explained. It had been the longest year of her life, thanks to him. From the first day they'd walked into Mrs. Barr's classroom and he'd been assigned the seat behind hers, he hadn't stopped teasing her for a second. Whoopie cushions on her chair, fake worms down the back of her shirt . . . once he even tied her sneaker laces to the legs of her desk when she wasn't looking.

She'd more than gotten her revenge, but her weapons had been words, not stuff you could buy in a novelty store. Chris had been pudgy when he was eleven, the chubbiest kid in the class. Holly had made up all kinds of names for him: Fatty Franklin, 747 ('cause he was a "wide-body"), Wally the Whale, Belly Boy.

None of the names sounded all that clever now that she thought about them, but they'd done plenty of damage at the time. Kids in the class had laughed at Chris, and his light brown freckles had disappeared as his face turned red with embarrassment. None of her insults had stopped him, though. He'd given her grief right up until elementary-school graduation when he'd chased her around the school lawn after the ceremony. In her hurry to get away from him, she'd fallen into the mud, staining her new pink lace dress and getting a permanent smudge on her diploma.

Holly had been so relieved when Chris's father had sent him away to Dover Prep, an all-boys boarding school. She hadn't seen him since and had forgotten he was still on planet Earth. That's why it was so amazing that seeing him now brought back so much anger.

It wasn't just him, of course. It was everything his family had done to her family and her town. The Paiges had lost their house, Landon had become a tourist trap, and Holly's father had lost all his fight. He'd refused to run again for mayor even though everyone wanted him to. He'd stopped caring about everything except his family and his little carpentry shop in back of the house. "From now on, I'm only looking out for myself and my own," he always said. Holly could never forgive Chris or his family for that.

"You look a lot better than you did in sixth grade," Chris said, eyeing Holly approvingly, "though I kind of miss the pigtails."

Holly hated to admit it, but Chris looked a lot better, too. Gone were any traces of pudginess. Chris's body was long and lean, with muscular arms and legs and a well-developed chest. His blond hair was streaked with even lighter strands of gold, and his light blue eyes stood out sharply against his tan skin. Holly stared into his eyes and noticed there were marbly flecks of darker blue.

"I guess you've graduated by now," Holly said.

Chris nodded. "Just last week. I'm going to Yale in September."

Holly tried not to feel jealous. She'd always wanted to go to an Ivy League college. But before she could even apply, she had to study for her high-school equivalency test to make up all the work she'd missed last year. Even if she did get accepted to a top school, there was no way of knowing if she'd live until graduation. Still, she couldn't blame *that* on Chris or his family. And Chris had always been a good student. "Congratulations," she said sincerely.

"What about you?" Chris asked. "Where are you going?"

Holly bit her lower lip. She wasn't sure how to answer that question. "I'm not sure yet," she hedged. Then she quickly changed the subject. "I guess you'll be hanging out by the pool all summer."

"I wish," Chris said, rolling his eyes. "Actually, my dad's putting me to work at the resort. I'm the tennis pro."

"He should turn pro," Brett chimed in. "He was ranked number one in the Northeast in the National Juniors."

Holly was impressed. "Cool," she said.

"I think my father's more set on my getting a law degree than winning Wimbledon," Chris said, "and I can't do both."

He glanced out the window at the stores on the other side of Main Street. There was Deerfield's Barbershop, now run by old Mr. Deerfield's seventy-five-year-old son; Anderson's Bookstore with its display of used paperbacks on a revolving rack outside the front door; Ye Olde Sweet Shoppe with glass jars of colorful gumdrops, chocolate turtles, and licorice ropes.

"How's Landon?" Chris asked. "I've been home for the holidays and all, but I almost never get down here to the old town." He glanced over at Mr. Deerfield, who was slowly counting out his usual thirty-five-cent tip. "Looks like nothing's changed, though."

"Yeah," Brett agreed. "Except for The Mountain and one dinky little movie theater, there's *nothing* going on here. No clubs, no restaurants, nothing."

"There's a fruit stand half a mile down the road," the guy with the glasses said. "I guess we could always go there and watch the peaches rot."

"Or soak up the local color," Brett suggested, snickering as Mr. Deerfield slowly shuffled by. "I bet that guy was here when the Pilgrims landed."

Holly bristled. She'd just been joking about

Mr. Deerfield herself, but it was different coming from an out-of-towner. "I'm surprised you never studied American history in prep school," she said. "The Pilgrims settled in Massachusetts, not Vermont."

"Yeah, Brett, lay off," Chris said. "That's Mr. Deerfield. He used to cut my hair when I was a kid."

"How 'bout that guy over there, then," Brett said, pointing to Jay Lawrence, who was finishing the last of his omelette. "I'll bet he only changes his pants once a month."

Holly smiled. Brett obviously didn't realize that Jay Lawrence could have bought and sold Landon ten times over. But it was more fun *not* to point out his mistake.

"You know, guys, since you're new in town, I'm going to give you a little inside info," Holly said, leaning in closer to the table. "You know what's *really* fun to do around here?"

Chris, Brett, and the other guy looked up at her with interest.

"If you're really looking for adventure," Holly said, "try hiking up to the peak of Mount Landon. Then jump off the back side!"

"Hey, Holly, chill," Chris said. "These guys are just kidding around."

"I guess we don't have the same sense of humor," Holly snapped. "Now, I'd love to continue chatting, but I've got work to do. Can I take your order?"

Rather than clip their order to the kitchen window, Holly delivered it by hand to her mom, who was frying half a dozen eggs on the grill. Peg Paige, like Holly, had straight black hair, only hers had a single streak of white on the left side. Her eyes were green with a rim of brown around the iris. Like Holly, she was tall and slim.

"What's the matter, Hol?" her mother asked, looking anxiously into Holly's face. "You're not feeling tired, are you? I've told you, if you want to take a nap or go home, just do it. I can get somebody to cover for you."

"No, no, Mom," Holly said, handing her mother the order. "I feel fine. I just ran into someone I didn't want to see."

"Who?" her mother asked, swiping away some stray strands of hair that were falling in her eyes.

"Chris Franklin. Remember him?"

Mrs. Paige's eyes narrowed. "Bill Franklin's son? What's he doing here?"

Holly shrugged. "He's home from prep

school. And it looks like he's brought some of his school buddies with him."

Holly stood up on tiptoe to look out the kitchen window at Chris's booth. The three guys were talking and laughing and blowing straw wrappers at each other. Chris turned toward the kitchen, caught her eye, and smiled. Holly immediately moved away.

Chris wasn't half as obnoxious as he'd been in sixth grade, but he really hadn't changed much if he was hanging out with jerks like Brett and the other guy. If all they could do was make fun of Landon and the people who lived here, then why didn't they just stay away?

"You know what, Mom? I have an idea," Holly said. "A way to really clean this place up."

"Yeah?" Mrs. Paige asked. "What's that?"

"I think we should put a sign on the door," Holly said. "Preppies Keep Out!"

Breathing hard from her climb up the steep mountain road, June came up over a rise and stopped short as The Mountain Resort came into view. Though June had seen it half a dozen times, it never failed to amaze her with its size and elegance. Nestled amid towering pine and spruce trees, the hotel's main building was made of cream-colored stone with stately marble columns framing the huge wooden doors. On either side of the main building was a massive three-story wing that hugged the curve of the mountain before disappearing beneath the trees. Limousines and Rolls-Royces and Porsches lined the wide driveway in front of the entrance. Casually but expensively dressed people emerged from their cars as luggage-laden bellhops in cream-colored uniforms streamed from car trunks through the hotel entrance and back again.

June knew where the employees' entrance was, but she wanted to walk through those huge wooden doors, feel the oversized brass doorknob in her hand, step over the plush carpeting that filled the lobby. As June entered, she promised herself that one day she'd come here as a guest, not a servant.

The lobby was cavernous, with oil-painted cherubs floating through fluffy clouds on the ceiling three stories above her head. Behind a long mahogany counter, clerks in cream-colored suits politely and efficiently assigned people to their suites. There was no such thing as simply a "room" at The Mountain. All the suites had a living room, bedroom, bathroom, private Jacuzzi, and terrace overlooking the mountains, golf course, and pool in the back.

June checked her watch. It was one minute to nine, and she still had to find her way to Housekeeping, located at the very end of the West Wing in the basement. Pushing her way past brass luggage carts and blond babies in expensive strollers, June raced for the stairs.

The basement hallway seemed to stretch for miles. Panting and sweating, June raced past boiler rooms and laundry rooms and storerooms filled with boxes. She reached the gray metal door labeled HOUSEKEEPING at five after nine.

"You're late!" said a bony woman sitting behind a gray metal desk. She wore a cream-colored dress with a white apron over it. Her narrow face was softened by short brown curls but not by the stern expression in her gray eyes.

"Sorry, Mrs. Donnely," June said, pulling her T-shirt away from her damp chest and fluttering it to circulate some air.

Mrs. Donnely rose from her chair and headed for another door in the back of the small, spare office. "Not a great start," she warned. "We expect our staff to be responsible and on time."

June winced. Had her father and Mrs. Donnely been chatting in the time it took her to get here? And what was the big deal? Five minutes wasn't *that* late.

Mrs. Donnely disappeared through the back door and reappeared with a cream-colored maid's uniform on a hanger, covered in see-through plastic. It looked just like the one Mrs. Donnely was wearing. June noticed that the skirt was so long it would cover her knees. "This should be your size," Mrs. Donnely said. "I'll show you to the employee locker room where you can change."

After June had changed her clothes and locked away her knapsack, Mrs. Donnely took her upstairs to the third floor and unlocked the door to a huge closet. She wheeled out a large cart stacked with fluffy white towels, cleaning supplies, toilet paper, and a straw basket filled with tiny bottles of shampoo, conditioner, and sweet-smelling bars of soap. An empty canvas bin was attached to one end of the cart.

"That bin is for dirty linens," Mrs. Donnely instructed, wheeling the cart down the plush carpet inlaid with a border of crimson roses. Farther down the hall, at regular intervals, identical carts were parked outside other doors. Mrs. Donnely paused at the first door on her left and pulled out a plastic card with holes punched in it. Sliding the card into a slot in the door, she turned the brass doorknob and entered the room. "Bring the cart," she instructed June.

June gasped when she saw the inside of the suite. Though she'd expected it to be large and beautifully furnished, she hadn't expected this. She and Mrs. Donnely stood in a marble-floored entrance hall. On the left wall, a huge vase of fresh flowers stood on a gilt table with curlicued legs. Straight ahead was a doorway leading to a living room that looked to be at least forty feet by forty feet, filled with antique French furniture, gold-framed oil paintings, and an expensive-looking Persian rug.

On the right wall was a door leading to a master bedroom. The king-sized bed had an intricately carved wooden frame with a canopy overhead. The tapestry bedspread was turned down, revealing rumpled white sheets. Silk-upholstered chairs and love seats were scattered around the room.

Mrs. Donnely wheeled the cart through the bedroom to another door. Inside, June could see a vast bathroom with white tiles on the walls and floor. Sunlight poured in through the gauzy white window curtains. A raised platform with a Jacuzzi filled one corner. A freestanding bathtub with clawed feet stood in another with a glass-doored shower stall next to it. The third wall had a toilet and large pedestal sink with brass knobs. Brass lighting fixtures were mounted on either side of the sink.

"Wow . . ." June breathed. Forget the rest of the hotel. She could spend the rest of her life right here in this bathroom and be perfectly happy.

Mrs. Donnely handed June a scrub brush and a can of powdered cleanser. "Lesson number one," she said. "How to scrub a toilet."

Chapter Four

Pock!

The fluorescent yellow tennis ball sailed over the net, over Chris's head, and landed outside the baseline on the red clay court.

"Try it again," Chris said, serving gently to Hilary's backhand.

The muscular blond girl, her pale blond hair pulled off her face by a white stretchy headband, again hit the ball with too much force.

Pock!

The ball was low this time, hitting the net on Hilary's side and dribbling down to the court.

"Unh!" Hilary cried in frustration. "What am I doing wrong?"

"Like I said before, go *easy*," Chris instructed her. He held out his own racket and swung it smoothly to demonstrate a backhand shot. "Flow with the ball, don't try to kill it."

Hilary nodded and wrinkled her forehead. "I know you're right. I'll work on it."

Chris checked his watch. Their hour was up. And none too soon. He'd been under the blazing hot sun for four hours straight, his head was beginning to hurt, and he was dying for a drink of water. "We'll try it again next week," he said. "Meanwhile, keep practicing."

Hilary nodded and walked toward her bag, which sat on a wooden bench at the side of the tennis court. Grabbing her towel, she mopped her sweat-soaked face.

"See you," Chris said, heading for the men's locker room.

"Hey, Chris, hold on a sec." Hilary jogged around the net and easily caught up with him. "Do you have plans for dinner tonight?"

"Just eating with my family, I guess." Every night during the summer, Chris and his parents ate at their own table in the Main Dining Room of the hotel, often inviting distinguished guests to join them. It was sort of like the captain's table on a cruise ship.

Hilary's face grew eager. "Well, maybe you and I could get our own table."

Chris kept his eyes down as he figured out how to answer. Hilary was a nice enough girl and he wouldn't mind eating with her, but it wasn't as simple as that. Chris's father had been trying for years to push Hilary and him together. Hilary's father was a bigwig lawyer down in Washington, D.C., and a friend of Chris's uncle Ron, who worked for the Justice Department. Chris knew his father was hoping that someday, after Chris had become a senator or congressman himself, he'd marry Hilary and form a political family dynasty like the Kennedys.

It was a glamorous picture of the future, but Chris wasn't sure that was what he wanted. He enjoyed tennis more than politics, though it was really too late for him now to get on the professional tennis circuit. Chris wasn't sure what he *did* want, but sometimes he fantasized about acting professionally. He'd starred in a play at Dover and had actually gotten good reviews in the school paper. And he loved stepping outside his own life and seeing the world through someone else's eyes. It was the perfect escape.

"Uh, I don't know, Hilary," Chris said. He didn't want to hurt her feelings, but he didn't want to encourage his father's plan, either. "Can I get back to you in a little while?"

Hilary smiled energetically. "Sure," she said. "Suite 303."

"Got it."

Hilary bounded away to the other side of the court. Chris passed out of the bright sunlight into the shaded walkway that led to the men's locker room.

"Chris!"

Chris blinked in the shadows. His eyes hadn't adjusted yet to the dimmer light so he didn't recognize the silhouette of the approaching figure.

"Was that Hilary Durham I saw you talking to?" the silhouette asked, getting closer. Now Chris could make out the broad shoulders, the proud head, the fading blond hair combed neatly over the beginnings of a bald spot. The tall man wore khaki pants and a spotless white polo shirt with The Mountain's logo over his heart.

"Hi, Dad," Chris said. "Yeah, that was her."

"That was *she*," his father corrected him. Bill Franklin was a stickler for good grammar the way he was about everything else. "How'd the lesson go?"

"Pretty good," Chris said. "She's still trying too hard, though."

"Nothing wrong with trying hard," Mr. Franklin said. "The girl takes after her father. Did you hear she got into Harvard?"

Hilary hadn't mentioned it, but Chris's father had at least five times. Just as he'd mentioned that Hilary was planning to go to law school as her father had and join her father's law firm in Washington.

"Yeah, Dad," Chris said, heading for the water fountain by the locker-room entrance. He let the icy water splash over his hot, red face, then stream down his parched throat. All he wanted right now was to take a shower and put on some dry, clean clothes.

"I've invited Hilary and her parents to join us for dinner tonight," Chris's father said, "so wear the new suit I got you, not that ratty old blazer. Got it?"

Chris lifted his wet face. It looked like there was no getting around it. He was having dinner with Hilary tonight whether he wanted to or not. "Yes, sir," he said.

"And maybe you should come prepared with a list of questions," Mr. Franklin said. "This is your opportunity to ask Mr. Durham

about politics, life in Washington, find out
about the law firms down there. . . ."

"I thought it was dinner, not a job interview," Chris protested.

Mr. Franklin clapped an arm around Chris's
shoulder. "You've got to take advantage of
every opportunity. That's what's made our family so successful. My grandfather ran a railroad
and made millions during the Depression. My
father inherited it all and didn't have to work a
day in his life, but did he kick back and relax?"

"No," Chris said. He knew his part of this
speech. He'd heard it so many times before.
"Your father invested the money in a chain of
department stores and increased his invest-
ment a hundred times over."

"That's right," Mr. Franklin said. "And what
did *I* do? Did I ride on my father's coattails?"

"No," Chris said. "You opened this hotel.
The largest resort in the state, and the most
profitable in the Northeast."

"Right," his father said. "And you've got
more talent and promise than any of us. With
our money and your brains, there's nothing
you can't do. You could run this country if you
put your mind to it."

What if I don't want to run the country? Chris

wanted to say, but of course he couldn't. When Bill Franklin made up his mind, there was no stopping him. And it was useless to try. Look what had happened to Chris's sister, Blaire. Their dad had been pushing Blaire toward law school and politics, too, only Blaire had decided she'd rather be a musician. Though she'd been valedictorian of her class at the Wainscott School, Blaire had skipped out on the graduation ceremonies. She ran off to San Francisco, where she'd started her own rock and roll band, Preppie Goes Berserk.

Chris had been secretly proud of his sister for standing up to their father. But Mr. Franklin had been furious. He'd cut off Blaire without a cent and refused to talk to her. It had been two years since Blaire ran away, and Mr. Franklin didn't seem to be softening his position one bit. As far as he was concerned, he had no daughter. Chris knew the same thing would happen to him if he ever tried to go against his father's plans.

"I guess I'll see you at dinner," Chris said quietly, heading for the locker room.

Inside, he headed straight for the showers. Peeling off his sweaty clothes, he stepped under the cool spray. *Nothing wrong with trying hard. You've got to take advantage of every opportunity. That's what's made our family so successful. You could run this country if you put your mind to it.* Chris let the water pound down on his head, trying to drown out the echoes of his father's voice.

If you're really looking for adventure, try hiking up to the peak of Mount Landon. Then jump off the back side! Chris laughed as he remembered how Holly had put down Brett and Hadley at the diner. They'd definitely deserved it. Just because she was a waitress was no reason for them to treat her so rudely. And even if Landon was a slow little town, they didn't have to act like such snobs.

On the other hand, Holly hadn't been too nice to them, either, with her cracks about prep school. She was still the same Holly Paige he remembered from sixth grade, with a sharp tongue and put-down for everybody. The same Holly Paige he'd had a crush on since the first day he'd ever seen her in Mrs. Barr's classroom. Only, he'd never had the nerve to tell her. That was why he was always picking on her and pulling her hair and pouring itching powder down her back. It was the only way he knew of, back then, to express his feelings. And she'd been so mean to him. Fatty Franklin. 747. The names still smarted even though Chris had lost all his excess weight years ago. On the other hand, she was just getting back at him for playing all those tricks on her.

Chris had always remembered Holly's dark pigtails and mischievous eyes and the way her nose crinkled when she smiled. But she was even prettier now. Her slender body had grown curvy and her hair hung like silk down her back. Most of all, she made him laugh. Chris hadn't met a girl in a long time who could do that.

But what was he thinking? He wasn't getting hung up on her again, after all these years, was he? This wasn't grade school, where you could show a girl you liked her by putting a frog in her desk. They were grown up now, and they were from two totally different worlds. If they hadn't known each other from grade school, Chris would never have even known a girl like her. Chris laughed trying to picture Holly in her waitress uniform sitting at his parents' table in the Main Dining Room. No way on earth that would ever happen.

Chapter Five

June took one last look at herself in the full-length mirror of the ladies' locker room. Her black bikini showed off the tan she'd been working on every day in the backyard and emphasized her rounded figure. June wasn't slim like Holly, but she was healthy looking with a body that got whistles every time she walked down Main Street. The wig looked good, too. June had always wanted to be a redhead. Pulling the wig forward a little, June put on her sunglasses. Perfect. Even if Mrs. Donnely happened to walk by the pool (and June knew she wouldn't because at this very moment she was eating her lunch in that dank little office in the basement), there was no way she'd recognize her.

Grabbing one of the neatly stacked towels from a basket on the floor, June slung her knapsack over one shoulder and hurried toward the door that led out to the pool. She only had half an hour before she had to report back to Mrs. Donnely, so she didn't have any time to waste. Pushing open the door, June emerged into the bright sunlight and stared in awe.

The turquoise pool covered half an acre. Irregularly shaped, fake rocks formed its curving border. A rope bridge spanned one narrow section of the pool. Farther back, more fake rocks formed a tall archway over another section of the pool. A giant waterfall flowed over these rocks, crashing down into the water below. Behind the waterfall, June could see a distant waterslide with more twists and turns than Annie's Krazy Straw.

Chaise lounges with cream-and-white striped cushions ringed the pool. More than half were filled with tan, toned men and women, reading paperbacks, sunbathing, or ordering food and drinks from the bikini-clad waitresses.

June was so hot from her morning of scrubbing toilets and vacuuming Persian rugs that she wanted to jump right into the pool and

cool off, but she couldn't because of her wig.
And she didn't have time anyway. She had to
hone right in on a guy and get to work.

Ambling slowly past the chaise lounges,
June looked for a young guy who was by himself or with other guys. She certainly didn't
want to hit on someone else's boyfriend or husband! She passed a young couple holding
hands as they napped. A mother was spreading
suntan lotion on her little girl's back. Two fat
old men wearing bathing trunks and smoking
cigars played cards on the table between their
lounges.

Up ahead there were a couple of young
guys by the edge of the pool, trying to push
each other into the water. June paused to
watch, but kept going once she realized they
were only about fourteen years old. She
wanted a college man.

"Excuse me," said a deep voice right behind
her. "You seem lost. Can I help you?"

June turned around. A tall, well-built young
man with glossy black hair and chiseled features
looked down at her with a friendly smile. He
wore baggy blue bathing trunks and a T-shirt
that said "Dover Prep." Well, maybe he wasn't in
college yet, but he was definitely close enough.

"I was just looking for a place to sit down. Where are *you* sitting?" she asked flirtatiously.

The guy grinned and pointed to a lounge nearby covered with a multicolored beach towel and a canvas beach bag at the foot. "Right there," he said. "And it looks like you're in luck." There was an empty lounge right next to it.

June spread her towel over the empty lounge and tried to arrange herself on it as gracefully as possible. The guy plunked himself down beside her and pulled a small transistor radio out of his beach bag. "Hope you don't mind some tunes," he said, turning on the radio to a rock station.

"Not at all," June said, bobbing her head to the beat of heavy metal. It wasn't her favorite music, but who cared? In less than five minutes, she'd bagged a live one. She was on her way.

"My name's Brett," the guy said, extending his hand. His fingers were long and lean, and his grip was strong as he shook June's hand.

"Lucia," June said. She'd read that name once, in a book about a rich girl who went to boarding school.

"Nice to meet you," Brett said. "You want to order some lunch?"

June hadn't eaten since her half a bowl of soggy cereal. She was starving but she didn't have much money with her, only five dollars. She wasn't sure how much food cost here, but it was probably more than she had. "Maybe just something to drink," she suggested.

"Aw, c'mon," Brett said. "I'm having a BLT and fries. Go for it. I'll charge it to my parents' suite."

"Well . . ." June's stomach gurgled so loud, she was afraid Brett could hear it over the sounds of the waterfall and kids splashing in the pool. "Sure," she said. "I'll have the same."

After Brett had flagged down a waitress, he turned back to her. "So, Lucia," he said. "What suite are you in?"

June thought quickly of the rooms she'd cleaned that morning. Number 319 had been empty, so it was probably a safe number to choose. "319," she said.

Brett grinned broadly. "What a coincidence! We're right across the hall. 322!"

June's stomach gurgled again, and she flung her arms across it. "Neighbors," she said, trying to sound enthusiastic. She should have thought out this part more carefully. She

should have told him she didn't remember her
room number. Not only would Brett discover
her lie if he knocked on the door of 319, but
room 322 was also one of the rooms June was
supposed to clean!

Maybe it would be a smart move to say her
good-byes now, before she got any deeper into
this lie. She'd find another guy on the other
side of the pool and get it right next time. June
started to rise, but Brett placed a warm hand on
her arm, sending tingles all through her body.

"What's the matter?" he asked.

June wavered. Maybe she could tell Brett
her parents had switched rooms. Maybe he
wouldn't recognize her without the wig and
sunglasses. And he was sooooooo sexy. June
sank back against the cushions. "Nothing," she
said. "Just getting comfortable."

"You feel pretty comfortable to me," Brett
said, letting his fingers brush up her arm toward her shoulder.

June closed her eyes and sighed. Her plan
was working perfectly, and it had been so easy!
Now Brett was pursuing her. Any minute now,
he'd ask her out to dinner. June already knew
what she'd wear to the Main Dining Room. A
black strapless dress she'd bought last year at a

thrift shop in Burlington, very simple and elegant, with her mother's pearl necklace and Holly's pearl earrings.

"Where are you from?" Brett asked.

Okay, maybe it wouldn't be *that* easy. There would have to be a few more lies before June closed the sale. But at least these lies had been rehearsed. "Boston," she said. June had a first cousin in Boston whom she talked to all the time and had visited twice. June figured she knew enough about the city to survive detailed questioning. "You?" she asked.

"Manhattan," he said. "But my family summers here every year."

My family summers, springs, winters, and falls here, June thought with a smile. "And what does your father do?" she asked.

"He works on Wall Street."

"And your mom?"

Brett laughed. "She does a lot of charity work," he said. "Or, at least, that's what she tells people. Mostly, she just attends a lot of black-tie events to benefit AIDS or the homeless or Famine Relief."

June nodded, hoping she looked like she had this sort of conversation all the time.

"And your parents?" Brett asked. "What do

they do?"

"My father's in construction," June said. This wasn't really a lie. Tom Paige constructed bookcases and tables and chairs and had even made a staircase once. "And my mother's in the restaurant business," June added.

"Cool," Brett said.

A waitress appeared and placed two bacon, lettuce, and tomato sandwiches on the table between them, followed by a basket of french fries and two sodas. Brett quickly signed his name and filled in his room number.

June took a big bite of her sandwich. It tasted better than any BLT she'd ever eaten at her mother's diner. June studied the sandwich closely, trying to figure out what made it special. The bread wasn't white toast but thick, whole-grain bread with little nutty seeds in it. The bacon wasn't fatty strips but thick slabs of Canadian bacon, more like ham. And the tomatoes were deep red, not half-green the way her mother usually served them.

"So, Lucia," Brett said, sipping Coca-Cola through a straw. "How long are you here for?"

"All summer," June said truthfully.

"That's great!" Brett said. "We'll have to hang out together."

June smiled as she grabbed a french fry. "I think that can be arranged." As she raised the french fry to her mouth, she noticed the time on her watch. It was already five minutes to one! She had to report to Mrs. Donnely at one o'clock. There was no way she could change back into her clothes and get back downstairs by then. But she had to try.

"Uh, Brett," June said, jumping up, "I'm really sorry, but I totally forgot. I've got to meet my parents. We're going"—June racked her brain for some classy-sounding activity—"antiquing! But thanks for lunch."

"I'll knock on your door," Brett said.

June smiled weakly. "Sure," she said. Casting a longing look at her BLT, June grabbed her towel and raced for the ladies' locker room.

Chapter Six

"Dancin' in Chicago . . . down in New Orleans . . ."

Holly sang along with the car radio as she drove home from her Monday checkup with Dr. Frazier. For the third month in a row, he'd given her a clean bill of health. No pain, no swelling, no fever, no fatigue, and all her blood tests were normal.

Holly turned her parents' dented station wagon off the rural highway onto a narrow road that curved past The Mountain. A cool breeze blew her hair straight back, and she breathed in the fresh smell of mountain pine. The sun was shining brightly overhead with just a few puffy clouds skidding by over the mountaintop.

Holly knew she had every reason to celebrate. But she couldn't let herself get too hopeful. Her lupus was in remission *for now*. There was still no guarantee for the future. Her condition could change at any time.

It was hard on such a beautiful sunny day to imagine herself dead, cold, alone in a box in the ground. Meanwhile, her family and friends would go on with their lives. Time would pass, and the only proof she'd ever existed would be a gravestone amid hundreds, thousands of others scattered over the rolling foothills of Mount Landon. A passerby might see her name on the stone, notice the dates, and wonder about a girl who'd died so young. Then the passerby would keep walking and not give it another thought.

An oncoming car, going too fast along the narrow two-lane road, shot past just inches away from Holly's car, its horn blaring. Holly laughed, shaking the morbid image of her gravestone out of her head. This near-collision proved there were no guarantees for *anybody's* future. She could get into a car accident. She could be hit by a bolt of lightning. Anything could happen to anybody, sick or not. So what was the point of worrying? It *was* a beautiful day, and it *was* good news, so Holly was going to enjoy herself.

"Everywhere around the world there'll be dancin' . . ."

Holly tapped on the steering wheel and bopped her head in time to the music. Up ahead, she saw a girl walking alone along the edge of the road, carrying a knapsack. As Holly got closer, she realized it was June. June must have just finished her first day of work at The Mountain. Holly pulled up alongside her sister and reached across the front seat to roll down the passenger window.

"Going my way?" she joked.

June grinned and hopped in the car. "Perfect timing," she said, throwing her knapsack into the backseat. "You coming from Dr. Frazier? What did he say?"

"So far so good," Holly said. "Everything's normal."

June shrieked and threw her arms around her sister. "That's great!"

Holly smiled at her sister's enthusiasm. "And how was your first day of work?" she asked, putting her foot on the accelerator.

"Not bad if you like menial labor," June said. "Let's see, I scrubbed eight toilets, dusted twenty antique Chinese vases, and stuffed about five hundred pillows into pillowcases.

You wouldn't believe how many pillows there are. At least a dozen on every bed!"

"That's the good life," Holly said wryly.

June shook her head. "For them, anyway. But it wasn't a total waste of time. I'm making progess with my plan."

"Uh-oh." Holly had already heard about June's plan and had even gone into Burlington with her sister to help pick out the wig. Not that she totally approved. It was foolish of June to think some rich guy was going to sweep her off her feet and take her away from Landon. That just happened in fairy tales.

And June still had two more years of high school. No way their parents would let June leave even if her fantasy *did* come true. Most of all, Holly firmly believed that a person should change her own life, not wait for someone to change it for her. But these were things June would have to figure out for herself.

"What happened?" Holly asked. "Did you meet someone?"

June fell back against her seat and sighed deeply. "He's sooooo cute!" she swooned. "Tall, black hair, high cheekbones, great build . . . like some artist sculpted him out of marble."

"Sounds great," Holly said, bearing left at a

fork in the road that led downhill. "What's his name?"

"Brett," June said. "I didn't catch his last name."

Holly looked out of the corner of her eye at her sister. Could this be Chris's friend, the guy she'd met at the diner this morning? "He wasn't wearing a Dover Prep T-shirt by any chance, was he?" Holly asked.

June turned to Holly in surprise. "Yeah! How did you know?"

Holly frowned. "I served him breakfast this morning. I'd stay away from him if I were you. He's a total snob. He snapped his fingers at me like I was his personal slave."

"Well, he was nice to me," June insisted. "He even bought me lunch."

Holly made a right onto Main Street, past the old maple tree that bore the scars of Mr. Deerfield's '62 Rambler. "He might not have been so nice to you if he knew you were a maid."

"And he's not going to find out," June pleaded. "You're not going to tell anybody, are you? It'll ruin everything!"

"Of course not!" Holly said. "I would never give away your secret. You know that. I'm just saying you probably don't want to get close to somebody who treats people so badly. He'll just do the same thing to you. And what if you get caught? You'll lose your job!"

"I know," June said. "But I'll be careful." June sank into the seat cushions and stared out the window as they drove past Harry's Homemade Ice Cream Parlor, the tiny redbrick post office, Deerfield's Barbershop, Peg's Diner, and the Five & Dime with its dusty window display of carpet sweepers, thermoses, laundry baskets, and cheap plastic toys. "What was Brett doing at the diner, anyway?" she asked.

Holly laughed. "You mean when he wasn't ordering me around and criticizing the food?"

"Okay, okay," June said. "I'm getting the picture."

"Actually, it was kind of funny," Holly said. "He was eating breakfast with some of his preppy friends, and you'll never guess who one of them was."

"Do I know any preppies?" June asked. "Not that I wouldn't like to."

"You might not remember him," Holly said. "I'll give you a hint. He was in my sixth-grade class at Landon Elementary School and he used to drive me *crazy*!"

June sat up and her eyes twinkled. "He was fat, right? Blond hair?"

Holly nodded.

June scrunched up her face, trying to remember. "What did you used to call him? Wally the Whale?!"

"And Fatty Franklin," Holly confirmed. "Only, he sure isn't fat anymore. I guess we'll just have to call him Chris."

"Is he still as obnoxious as he was in sixth grade?"

Holly was going to say yes, but then she remembered the way Chris had defended Mr. Deerfield when his friends were making fun of him. She remembered the intensity in Chris's eyes as he'd stared at her, his approving smile as he looked her up and down. She smiled as she thought about how he'd flirted with her. "I guess he's not so bad . . ." she conceded.

"I guess not," June said, laughing. "From the look in your eyes, I'd say he's not too bad at all!"

Holly turned abruptly toward her sister. "What are you talking about?"

"I've seen that look before," June said. "Like, this afternoon in the mirror, right after I met Brett!"

Holly snorted. "Oh, no!" she protested. "You

like Brett. I just said Chris wasn't as bad as he used to be."

June smiled and folded her arms across her chest. "Say whatever you like. I can read body language. And you like him. I say go for it."

"And I say you're crazy! He's a *Franklin*, remember?"

Holly turned off Main Street onto their street, Rutland Road. The road swooped down past a dairy farm with grazing cows, then up again to the Paiges' small, two-story house. The house, covered with aluminum siding, was absolutely plain and absolutely symmetrical. A screened, white front door sat exactly in the middle of the bottom floor with a square window on either side. On the second floor were two more square windows, directly above the windows on the first floor.

Holly saw that the front door was open and four faces peered through the screen. It was Holly's dad, mom, Annie, and Sal. They started waving frantically when they saw the car pull up the driveway, and Holly's mom ran out to the driveway.

"Who cares if he's a Franklin?" June whispered as Holly shifted the car into park. "He's loaded!"

"Can we please stop talking about Chris?" Holly asked. "I don't want Mom and Dad to hear."

Mrs. Paige poked her head through Holly's open window, her face full of anxiety. "What did the doctor say?" she asked without even saying hello.

Holly gave her mother a thumbs-up. "Still in remission," she said. "Everything looks good for now."

"She's fine, Tom," Mrs. Paige sang out.

Holly's father ran toward them, his tired face lighting up. "I knew it!" he shouted. "Our baby's fine!"

"I didn't say fine, Mom," Holly objected. Much as she hated to see the fear and worry on her parents' faces, she hated this even more, this denial that anything was wrong. It was like they thought if they pretended she wasn't sick anymore, the lupus would go away.

Mrs. Paige opened the car door and Sal and Annie ran toward Holly, smothering her with hugs and kisses.

"Hey, guys!" Holly said, breathing in their scent of sugary jawbreakers, fresh grass, and bicycle grease.

"Did you hear, Holly?" Sal shouted. "We made

it! We're finalists in The New England Mountain Bike contest! They just called. Maybe we'll get to star in the ad *and* win a free mountain bike!"

"We have to go there tomorrow to get our pictures taken with the other finalists," Annie added. "We think we have twice as good a chance of winning 'cause there's two of us. Boy, I could really use a new bike. Mine's all worn out."

Annie spoke the truth. She and Sal were constantly riding the hilly roads on their bikes, which were not only old but getting too small for them. But now that their parents were in so much debt to pay Holly's medical bills, they couldn't afford to buy the twins new ones. Holly felt guilty that her illness had cost everyone in her family so much pain and sacrifice.

"Good luck, you guys," she said. "I'll put in a good word for you with Jay."

"Dinner's on the table," said Peg Paige as Holly and her sister got out of the car. "I made your favorite—chicken parmigiana and lemon meringue pie."

Just in case it was my Last Supper, Holly couldn't help thinking. Then she got mad at herself. She'd just decided she wasn't going to worry or think morbid thoughts. And she planned to stick to that.

"Great!" Holly said with enthusiasm. "I'm starved!"

At the dinner table, after Holly had recounted every last detail of her doctor visit, her dad turned to June.

"And how did those Franklins treat you?" he asked. "Did they walk all over you the way they walked all over this town?"

June pursed her lips. "I didn't even see any Franklins," she said. "It's just a job, Dad. Can't you leave it at that?"

"That reminds me, Tom," Holly's mother said. "One of *those Franklins* came into the diner this morning and started making trouble."

Holly's father's face grew red. "Which one?"

"The son," Mrs. Paige said. "Holly said he insulted her . . ."

"I didn't say that," Holly cut in. "It was his friends, really."

Tom Paige wasn't listening. "Like father, like son," he muttered. "Thinks he owns this town. Thinks he can walk in anywhere he likes and call the shots." He pounded his fist on the table.

"It wasn't like that!" Holly protested.

"You want me to talk to the sheriff?" Tom Paige asked his wife. "Maybe there's some legal

action we can take. At least keep them out of
your diner . . ."

"Dad . . ." Holly regretted ever mentioning
Chris to her mother this morning. Not that she
took seriously her father's threat to call the
sheriff. But both her parents were blowing this
thing way out of proportion. Chris hadn't been
rude to her at all. In fact, he'd been nicer to
her than she'd been to him.

Holly was beginning to regret the way she'd
insulted him and his friends. He hadn't deserved it. He wasn't the same person he'd been
in sixth grade. And Holly had just let herself
get carried away with this Paige-Franklin feud
the way her father was doing right now. But
she couldn't take back her words, and she
couldn't change history. Paiges hated
Franklins, and vice versa.

Anyway, what difference did it make? Chris
lived up on The Mountain, and she never went
there. Their paths would never cross again.
Holly resolved not to spend one more minute
thinking about Chris Franklin.

Chapter Seven

The sun beat down on Holly's head, making her uncomfortably warm despite her wide-brimmed straw hat. Or maybe she was hot because she was wearing a long-sleeved shirt even though it was eighty degrees out. Dr. Frazier had warned her to protect herself from the sun at all times, so Holly always wore a hat, sunglasses, long sleeves, and sunscreen whenever she went outside. Holly knew it looked ridiculous, but it was better than getting those horrible rashes on her face again.

Or maybe she was hot because, for the first time in over a year, she was actually getting some real exercise. Holly had felt so good when she woke up this morning that she'd decided it was time to get back into shape. She

couldn't jog or bicycle the way she used to because she had to avoid stress, but Dr. Frazier
had said it was okay to walk.

Holly had taken off about an hour ago, hiking
along the path that wound its way up the side of
Mount Landon. Ferns and berry bushes lined
the dirt path, and white-tailed deer rustled in the
trees beyond. Far below, the Winooski River
stretched westward toward Lake Champlain.
Holly could see Landon, too, tinier than ever
from this distance. It looked like a toy town from
a model train set.

Taking off her hat, Holly paused to fan her
face. She was getting thirsty. Just up ahead was
a clearing with a paved road running through
it. That road might get her down the mountain
faster than going back the way she'd come.
Jamming her hat onto her head, Holly headed
for the clearing.

It turned out not to be a clearing at all. It
was a golf course. The lush green lawn spread
for acres across the gently sloping side of the
mountain. Middle-aged men in plaid pants
drove golf carts around scattered ponds, sand
traps, and clumps of trees.

Beep beep! The sound was coming from behind her. Holly turned to see another golf cart

loaded with two elderly couples coming her way. As Holly stepped aside to let it pass, she read the logo stenciled on the side of the golf cart: THE MOUNTAIN RESORT.

Holly laughed. In the ten years since The Mountain had been built, she'd never been up here. This was the last place she'd expected to end up today. The paved road led downward, lined by tall leafy trees. Holly followed it, grateful for the shade. Ahead of her a curving, cream-colored building seemed to stretch forever. In front of it was the largest swimming pool Holly had ever seen. Coming up closer, on her right, was a high chain-link fence with half a dozen tennis courts behind it.

Pock! Pock!

Two little girls batted a tennis ball back and forth over the net, sending each other running wildly all over the court to return the ball. The next court was empty. Holly suddenly remembered that Chris had said he was a tennis instructor at his father's resort. Wouldn't it be weird if she ran into him here after everything that had happened? Of all the places her feet should bring her . . .

"Try it again, Mrs. Faulkner," said a young man in white shorts and white T-shirt on the next court. "Don't cut your stroke short. Step into the shot."

Holly's heart jumped. She knew that voice. It was Chris!

"Jill," said the woman on the other side of the net. "Call me Jill." She smiled at Chris in a more-than-friendly way. In her thirties, she was pretty and slim, with too much makeup and leathery tan skin.

Without answering, Chris expertly hit a ball right to her forehand. Jill gave the ball a little tap that didn't even get it as far as the net on her side. "Sorry," she said, smiling at Chris again. "Maybe if you came over here and showed me again."

No doubt about it. This woman was definitely flirting with Chris, and she was married! Not that Holly couldn't understand what this woman saw in him. His blond hair, damp with sweat, had separated into tousled curls. A pair of black Ray•Ban sunglasses topped his long, straight nose and strong jaw. His sweat-soaked shirt clung to his lean torso, showing off the well-defined muscles of his back.

Chris took a few running steps toward the net and leaped gracefully over it. "Okay, Mrs. Faulkner," he said patiently. "Just do what I do.

Bring your racquet all the way back and follow through . . ." As Chris turned to face the net, he noticed Holly. Tipping his sunglasses down, he looked over the top, then smiled. "Hey!" he said, waving.

Embarrassed, Holly waved back. She didn't know whether to keep walking or wait around to say hello. She didn't want Chris to think she was being rude again by leaving. On the other hand, she didn't want him to think she'd come by just to see him. It was a total coincidence that she'd happened to walk by here. She didn't want him to think she liked him, and she didn't want him to feel she was intruding on his property. Holly decided to keep walking.

Picking up the pace, she followed the road out of the shade onto an open stretch, leading down past the pool. The sun felt hotter than ever, like the temperature had gone up another ten degrees since she'd left the mountain path. Holly's mouth and throat felt so sandpapery dry, it was hard to swallow. And her legs suddenly felt so heavy.

Maybe if she just got out of sight of the tennis courts, she could find a little spot to rest, just for a minute, before making her way home. There was a tree a few yards ahead, on

the left. Holly slowly made her way toward it
and sank down, leaning against it. Holly shut
her eyes. Her head seemed to be pulsing in
time to the beat of her heart.

"You okay?"

Holly opened her eyes. Chris was looking
down at her, his blue eyes warm with concern.
He was still holding his tennis racquet.

"Sure," she said, swallowing with difficulty. "I
haven't exercised in a while. I guess I overdid it."

Chris knelt beside her. "Looked like you
were about to keel over." He put a comforting
hand on her shoulder.

Holly liked the way his touch made her feel.
Warm, protected, safe. But wait a minute. This
was Chris Franklin she was talking about! The
guy who used to pull her chair out from under
her in Mrs. Barr's class whenever she went to
sit down.

"I'm fine," she insisted. "Just a little out of
shape."

Chris's eyes traveled from her face down the
length of her body. Holly almost *felt* his eyes
touch her, like a soft caress—a soft, *exciting* caress. "You don't look out of shape to me," he
said softly. Then he grinned. "But what's this
outfit you're wearing? Hat, sunglasses . . . you're

all covered up. Are you a spy or something?"

Holly laughed. "Or something." She didn't want to tell him about her lupus. It was much too heavy a subject to lay on him in a casual conversation. Anyway, she liked the fact that he *didn't* know she was sick. He was probably the first person she'd met in a long time who treated her like a normal person.

Holly was so tired of all the worried looks and false cheerfulness. *Oh, I'm sure you're going to be just* fine*! I've been reading about lupus, and they say you could live a* perfectly normal life*!* Holly also liked the fact that Chris didn't know she'd been the local "poster child" this past winter. All those "Save Holly" collection cups all over town. That would have made Chris think of her even more as some poor townie who had to beg for money to pay her bills.

No. Holly's mind was made up. There was no way she'd ever tell Chris she was sick. "Look," she said. "I'd better get home. Sorry I took you away from your lesson." Holly tried to rise, but she still felt so weak.

"I'll get you something to drink," Chris said. "You're probably overheated."

"No!" Holly protested, but Chris was already racing toward a low building beside the pool.

In less than three minutes, he was back with two tall, cold lemonades.

"Here," he said, handing one to Holly and dropping down to the grass beside her.

Holly's fingers wrapped around the frosty glass, and the ice cubes jingled. She'd be a fool to turn this down. Holly lifted the glass to her lips and let the sweet cool drink run down her parched throat. "Thanks," she said, smiling at Chris.

Chris smiled back, and Holly noticed that he had two dimples on one side of his mouth and none on the other. She was noticing so many sides of him she never would have dreamed existed two days ago. His kindness, his sense of humor, his wonderful manners . . . which reminded her. She still owed him an apology for her own rudeness.

"I'm sorry about what I said yesterday," Holly said, holding the frosty glass against her flushed cheek. "About preppies and jumping off the back of Mount Landon. I was way out of line. The customer's always right, right?"

Chris shook his head. "Brett and Hadley deserved it. They're a couple of boneheads. Just because they come from big cities they think they can put down our town."

Holly looked at Chris in surprise. "*Our* town? You don't really live here anymore, do you?"

"No," Chris admitted. "But I was born here, and this is where my family is, the place I come back to. The place where my memories are . . ." He gave Holly a veiled look, then laughed.

"What's so funny?" Holly asked.

Chris shook his head. "It's too embarrassing. You'll think I'm a total geek."

"What?" Holly asked, wondering why Chris would say that. No matter what he'd looked like or done in the past, no one could ever call him a geek now.

"Well, I owe you an apology, too," Chris said. "For what I did to you in Mrs. Barr's class."

Holly shrugged. "We were kids then. It doesn't matter now."

"But I never told you *why* I was always bothering you," Chris said. "I . . . um . . ."

"What?" Holly asked.

Chris cleared his throat, then spoke very quickly. "I had a major crush on you," he said. "But I was totally immature, so all I could do about it was pull your hair and make your life miserable."

Holly was floored. Never in a million years would she have expected Chris to say that. And from the way he was looking at her now, his blue eyes soft, his hand just inches from hers on the grass, she half-wondered if he *still* felt that way . . . and if she might be starting to feel that way, too.

"I—I should be heading back," Holly stammered. She felt her cheeks grow hot as she handed Chris her empty glass. "Thanks for the picnic. I had a great time. I've got the lunch shift at the diner, and I don't want to be late."

Chris hopped to his feet. "You want a ride? My Jeep's parked right over there." He pointed down the hill to a huge expanse of parking lot filled with expensive, shiny foreign cars.

"That's okay," Holly said. "It's not far."

Chris looked disappointed. "Well, come back any time. I'd be happy to give you a tour of the place."

Holly felt guilty enough that she'd ended up at The Mountain accidentally. She didn't think her parents would be too happy if she started coming back here on a regular basis. "Sure," she answered noncommittally, and started to walk away.

"Or maybe I'll stop by the diner," Chris called after her. "Your mom makes a great chili burger."

Holly looked back over her shoulder and smiled. Maybe Chris still *was* a little bit interested in her. But it couldn't be *serious* interest. It was one thing for Chris to like her when they were little kids and things like money and family and social position didn't matter. But things were totally different now. Chris was in a position to choose any girl he wanted—a prep-school graduate, a million-dollar heiress . . . certainly not someone like her.

"See ya," Holly said with a wave.

Chapter Eight

What a waste! June had a full-hour break for lunch, and she'd already spent the first half of it in a fruitless search for Brett. She'd walked all the way around the pool twice, but there was no sign of him. She'd wandered past the tennis courts, peeked in at the golf clubhouse, and scoped out the lobby, but he was nowhere to be found. And now he'd never see the preppy outfit she'd put together just for his benefit.

Last night, June had pulled every piece of summer clothing she had out of her closet and drawers and mixed and matched until she'd found the perfect combination. Her first day at The Mountain had already given her some pointers as to how the guests dressed. Lots of white, canvas sneakers without socks, casual sports shirts, even for women. Not too much jewelry. Just enough to look like you were rich but didn't have to advertise it.

June had found just the right pair of shorts— white and almost knee-length, but figure-hugging to show off her curvy hips. And she had a short-sleeved pink-and-white polo shirt that was a tiny bit snug after too many trips through the dryer. A pair of white Keds and, of course, her red wig and sunglasses completed the outfit. As June cruised once again past the cream-colored leather sofas in the lobby, she felt totally confident that she fit right in.

Up ahead, between a pair of giant stone urns, was a stairway leading up to the outside. A sign beside one of the urns said TERRACE CAFÉ. June hadn't tried that yet, and it *was* lunchtime. Maybe Brett was eating lunch. June took the stairs two at a time.

Surrounded by a stone wall, the outdoor terrace overlooked the golf course. Cream-and-white striped beach umbrellas topped round iron tables with scrolled legs. Casually dressed people sat in matching iron chairs with striped cushions. Waiters in cream-colored shorts and white polo shirts gracefully avoided each other as they carried heavy trays of sandwiches, chips, pickles, and soft drinks.

June scanned the tables, looking for a head of black shiny hair. Then she spotted Brett sitting with another guy at a table near the edge of the terrace. They were talking and laughing, and Brett had his feet up on an empty chair beside him.

June frowned. She hadn't counted on company while she worked on Brett, but she could still move this relationship along. Taking a deep breath, June walked slowly toward their table.

"Hey!" Brett called, spotting her immediately. "Cinderella!" He waved her over to his table.

June was startled. Sure, she'd spent the past four hours mopping marble floors, making beds, and scrubbing out sinks with Ajax, but how did Brett know that? Was he already onto her secret? Could he have somehow seen her when she was cleaning his room this morning? June had carefully checked to make sure no one was in the two-bedroom suite he shared with his parents. Even if he had seen her, there was no way he would have recognized her in her baggy maid's uniform.

Smiling nervously, June approached Brett and his friend. "Hi," she said.

Brett removed his feet from the empty chair and brushed it off with a napkin. "Sit down!" he said, a broad smile covering his perfect face. "Where've you been hiding?"

June relaxed a little. Brett didn't sound like someone who'd just discovered he'd been flirting with a maid.

"I've been . . . around," June said vaguely as she sank into the thick cushions of the chair. "But why'd you call me Cinderella?"

" 'Cause the clock struck yesterday and you ran away," Brett said. "Just disappeared. Hadley, here, was beginning to think I made you up."

The other guy grinned and rose, hand extended. "Hadley Pierce," he said in a friendly tone. Tall and skinny, he wore round glasses, and his light brown hair was slicked straight back.

"This is Lucia . . ." Brett paused. "I don't even know your last name."

Fortunately, June was prepared for this question. She'd made up a whole bunch of new stuff last night so she wouldn't be caught off guard again. In the same book about Lucia, the rich girl who'd gone to boarding school, there'd been a fancy hotel called The Chatsworth. June thought it had just the right sound. "Chatsworth," she said, shaking Hadley's hand.

"From Boston," Brett supplied.

"Any relation to Chuck Chatsworth?" Hadley asked. "He went to school with us. Lives on Beacon Hill."

June shook her head. "Sorry."

A waiter appeared at the table with two plates of sandwiches and placed them in front of Brett and Hadley. June wasn't as hungry today as she'd been yesterday. She'd eaten a huge breakfast just in case her search for Brett didn't include food. And much as she wanted to stick around, she didn't want Brett to think she expected him to buy her lunch again.

"I don't want to interrupt," she said, getting up. "Maybe I'll see you by the pool tomorrow."

"Don't be silly," Brett said, grabbing her arm and gently guiding her back down into her chair. Again, June felt a rush of blood shoot up her arm from the spot where he'd touched it. She felt warm all over even though it was cool here in the shade of the umbrella. "Don't you want to eat?" Brett asked as June sat back down. He grabbed a menu from the next table. "Come on. You got to have something."

June scanned the beige cardboard menu with its embossed gold letters and spotted bacon, lettuce, and tomato, under sandwiches. Her mouth started to water at the thought of the delicious sandwich she'd left unfinished yesterday. "How 'bout a BLT and a diet Coke?" she asked.

"You got it." Brett quickly flagged down the waiter and ordered for June.

"But this time, I'm paying for it," June insisted. She'd also come prepared today with plenty of money in her pocket. She didn't want Brett to think she was a sponge.

Brett waved away her words with his hand. "Let my dad pay," he said. "It's the least he can do."

"What do you mean?" June asked.

Brett sighed. "He was supposed to come up today and spend the week with my mom and me. But he canceled. Had to go to London or Brussels or someplace for a deal he's doing."

"That's too bad," June said.

"I guess I should be used to it by now," Brett said. "It happens all the time. Last summer when we were here he only made it up once for two days, then he got called away again."

June thought about her own dad, who was

constantly underfoot in their tiny house when he wasn't working in the small barn out back he'd converted into his carpentry shop. He was always giving orders and instructions or asking for a hand with some lumber he needed to unload off the back of the station wagon. He was always grumbling about The Mountain, asking questions about guys she was dating, and offering unwanted advice about what she should do with her life. In short, he was a pain in the butt. But for the first time she was beginning to appreciate the fact that he was always there.

"I'm sorry," June said sympathetically, patting Brett's hand, which rested on the table. "You must really miss him."

Brett's dejected look instantly brightened. "Yeah," Brett admitted, "but now I've got *you* to keep me company. And you're a lot cuter than my dad."

June's eyes were caught by the gleam in Brett's brown ones. His eyes promised so much—midnight swims under the waterfall in the hotel pool, drives along mountain roads in a hot Italian sports car, fancy dinners in the Main Dining Room here, or maybe even at some of the fancy places in Burlington. Who cared if sweeping and scrubbing were the price she had to pay to get close to him? It was all going to be worth it.

Hadley gobbled down the rest of his sandwich and pushed his seat back from the table. "I've got a golf game," he said. "Catch you guys later."

As Hadley took off, the waiter brought June her sandwich. She let her teeth sink into the crunchy whole-grain bread, salty bacon, and rich ripe tomato. She was in heaven. And now that Hadley was gone, she and Brett were alone.

"So, Lucia," Brett said, sliding his heavy chair a little closer. His bare tan leg was so close to hers that she could feel the warmth coming from it. He placed a hand on her thigh.

June put her sandwich down and smiled. Brett was obviously experienced, and though she thought he was moving fast, she didn't want him to think she couldn't handle his type.

"I'm not letting you get away again," Brett said. "How'd you like to have dinner with me tomorrow night?"

Bingo! Her plan was coming off flawlessly! June couldn't wait to tell Holly. But she tried not to let the excitement show on her face. "I think I'm free," she said calmly. "Where?"

"The Main Dining Room has pretty decent

food," he said. "I mean, for a local place. Of course, it's not New York . . . or Boston." He gave June a knowing look, as if they were two sophisticated people stuck against their will at this hole-in-the-wall little place.

June tried to mirror his look. "I guess it's the best we can do," she said. Then she panicked. Had she sounded *too* snobby, like she didn't appreciate his invitation? "But the Main Dining Room would be fine," she added enthusiastically. "I mean, it's not the food so much as who you're with."

Brett's fingertips found their way down to June's bare knee and rested there. "Exactly," he said. "Shall I meet you at your room? Suite 319, right?"

June gulped. A family had just checked into suite 319 this morning. If Brett knocked on her door, he'd find her out for sure. "Uh . . . good memory," she said, "but I'm going to be out with my family until then. Why don't I meet you at the restaurant?"

Brett looked wistful. "You do a lot of stuff with your family."

June nodded. That much was true, at least. Taking another bite of her sandwich, she noticed her watch. It was five minutes to one again. Time for her to turn back into a pumpkin. Mrs. Donnely had yelled at her yesterday for getting back late from lunch and had warned her not to let it happen again.

June took another big bite of her sandwich, and stood up. "I hate to do this . . ." she started to say.

"I know," Brett said with a sigh. "You've got to go."

"But I could meet you by the pool tomorrow," June suggested. "At lunchtime. That is, if you don't mind seeing me twice in one day."

Brett gave June a sexy grin. "I don't mind at all," he said, "especially the part of you I get to see by the pool."

"Meet you by the waterfall," June said. "Around noon?"

"I'll be there," Brett said.

June grabbed her sandwich. She couldn't bear to leave it there again, uneaten. "For the road," she explained, dashing away.

Chapter Nine

"There's a spot!" Sal cried excitedly late Tuesday afternoon. She pointed to a parking space in front of Jennifer's Antiques. "Quick, Holly! Before someone gets it!"

"No one's going to take it," Holly said, driving the station wagon right into the empty spot at the side of the dirt road. No one else was even *on* the side road that branched off Main Street. But Holly could understand why her little sister was so excited. Sal and Annie were about to get their pictures taken by a professional photographer, along with the other eight finalists of The New England Mountain Bike contest.

June, sitting beside Holly in the front seat, turned to look at Sal and Annie. "Let me check you out," she said, eyeing them critically. Holly turned around, too.

Sal and Annie's thick brown hair was tamed into neat braids that ran down the backs of their necks halfway to their waists. Over pink T-shirts, they wore identical overalls in different colors: Sal's was pistachio green, and Annie's was lavender. Their hopeful, rosy faces were scrubbed clean and shiny. Holly ached with love for them, for their enthusiasm, for how badly they wanted those mountain bikes.

She also couldn't help but think that this might be the last time she would drive them all somewhere. It hurt to think that she might not be around to experience all that life had to offer with each one of her sisters. That she wouldn't grow old with them.

"Let's go," she said, shaking off the feeling of gloom she always fought so hard to keep at bay, and opening the front door of the car. "Jay said five o'clock. It's two minutes to."

"And a Paige is never late!" Annie piped up.

"Except for June," Sal said.

June, too, opened her door. "Come on, movie stars," she grumbled, but Holly could tell she wasn't really mad. In fact, she'd never seen June so happy as when she'd gotten home from The Mountain this afternoon. Since they'd all had to rush over here for the photo session, June hadn't been able to give Holly any details, but she'd quickly whispered to Holly that she had good news about Brett. Holly had a feeling June would fill her in as soon as they got inside.

The girls crossed the street and found themselves right in front of The New England Mountain Bike Company Corporate Headquarters. At least, that's what it was called. It looked more like a large house than an office building. Four stories tall, the light blue shingled house had dark blue shutters and a peaked roof. There was a front porch with wicker furniture and rocking chairs. Holly smiled. It looked like this typical New England house had been here for ages, but she knew Jay had had it built just a few years ago. He'd said he wanted it exactly this way so his company wouldn't destroy Landon's small-town atmosphere.

Sal and Annie dashed up the three front steps and across the porch, flinging open the screen door that led inside. Holly and June followed and found themselves inside what looked like a large living room. Comfy sofas covered with rumpled slipcovers and flowered pillows were already filled with people, probably the other finalists. Various models of New England Mountain bikes hung on the walls like modern sculpture. Near the door was an old wooden desk with an elderly woman sitting behind it.

"May I help you?" she asked.

"Yes," Holly said, putting her arms around her little sisters. "These are Sal and Annie Paige."

"Ah, yes," the woman said, checking off something on a list. "You're here for the contest. Please have a seat and we'll call them when it's their turn."

Sal and Annie raced for an empty spot on one of the couches, but there was no room for Holly or June.

"Let's sit over there," June whispered, pointing to two cozy armchairs in a far corner. "It's more *private*."

Holly smiled. She knew she was about to hear about Brett. As she and June crossed the room, she glanced at the other finalists. There were men, women, some old, some young, a little boy, and a teenage girl reading a magazine.

Holly stopped short and stared in disbelief. June looked at her questioningly. Without daring to speak since the girl was only two feet

away, Holly just opened her eyes wider, hoping
June would know to take a closer look. June
did, and then her eyes popped open, too.

The girl wore wrinkled jeans, a boxy pink
shirt, and work boots. She wore no makeup,
and her straight, strawberry-blond hair was
pulled back off her face with a brown plastic
headband that looked like it came from the
Five & Dime on Main Street. She looked like
half the girls Holly had gone to school with,
like the girls who walked into the diner all the
time. Which was why it had taken Holly a second to realize who this girl was.

"Cynthia Dansby?" Holly asked.

Cynthia looked up and scowled when she
saw Holly. "*You're* not a finalist, are you?" she
asked.

"No," Holly answered. "But my sisters are."
She knew she was still staring, but she couldn't
help herself.

"What are you looking at?" Cynthia asked in
a nasty tone.

"Uh . . . nothing," Holly said. "It's just that
you look so . . . natural!"

June, who was standing right next to Holly,
giggled.

"I've got a lot of different looks," Cynthia

said. "It's part of being a professional model."

"Which you're not, yet," June pointed out.

Cynthia ignored June, looking pointedly back at her magazine. Holly pulled June over to the chairs in the corner.

"So *that's* what she looks like under all those layers of makeup!" June commented after they'd sat down.

"Shhhh," Holly warned. "She'll hear!"

June lowered her voice. "The big question is—where did she get those clothes? I've never seen her wear pants in my life!"

"*Wrinkled* pants," Holly emphasized. "She must have stayed up half the night to get just the right effect."

"What do you mean?"

Holly smiled because she'd figured it out as soon as she'd recognized Cynthia. "Jay said he wants someone who represents small-town values," she whispered. "Someone who'll look at home beside a mountain bike, The Spirit of the Mountains. Cynthia must have figured the only way to win this contest was to change her look."

"Looks like it worked," June observed. "But I'd be so mad if she won the bike away from Sal and Annie. She'd probably never even ride it."

"I know," Holly agreed. "I'm sure she's just

in the contest so she can star in the ad . . ."

". . . and model her way right out of this town," June said.

A young man in jeans and flannel shirt entered the reception area from a hallway in the back. "Sal and Annie Paige," he said, consulting a clipboard.

Sal and Annie jumped out of their seats. "We're here!" they shouted at the same time.

The man laughed. "Follow me, please."

"Good luck!" Holly called out. June gave them the thumbs-up.

After the twins had gone, June turned excitedly to Holly. "Brett asked me out!" she announced.

Holly had expected something like this. "When?" she asked.

"Tomorrow night. In the *Main Dining Room!* Can you believe it?"

"Sounds like everything's going according to plan," Holly admitted. Though she was happy for her sister, she still couldn't help feeling something was bound to go wrong. Either Brett would discover the truth about June or June would realize the truth about Brett.

June pouted. "Well, you could sound a *little* enthusiastic."

"I am," Holly said. "I just want you to be careful. You still don't know what he's really like."

"I know enough," June insisted. "So what about you and Chris? Did he show up at the diner again?"

Holly hesitated. She didn't want to tell her sister that she'd been up to The Mountain this morning or June would think she'd done it on purpose, just to see Chris. On the other hand, she was still feeling so confused about him. All afternoon she'd kept glancing at the door of the diner, hoping he'd walk in. She'd replayed their conversation over and over and felt again the shivers of excitement at the feel of his hand on her shoulder. She'd tried her best not to think about him, but it wasn't any use. She just *had* to talk about this with somebody.

"I didn't see him at the diner," Holly said, "but I sort of . . . ran into him this morning when I went for a walk."

June leaned in closer to Holly, her face alive with interest. "And?"

"Okay, I'll admit it," Holly said. "He *is* cute."

"Duh!" June said. "I've seen him at the tennis courts. He's *gorgeous*! So what happened? Did he ask you out or what?"

"Well, he offered to give me a ride home and he also said he'd give me a tour of The Mountain."

"That's great! When are you going to do it?"

"We didn't make any specific plans."

June was dumbfounded. "Why not?"

Holly's guilty look must have given June the answer.

"You mean you didn't encourage him? Holly, what's wrong with you?"

"Nothing!" Holly snapped. "Why *should* I encourage him? He's a Franklin. Mom and Dad might let you work at The Mountain, but I think that's as much contact as they'd let any of us have with that family."

"So don't tell them," June said. "They don't have to know."

"There's plenty of other reasons, too," Holly said. "I mean, I'm so busy. I've got to work at the diner . . ."

"No you don't," Holly pointed out. "Mom doesn't want you to work, remember? She wants you to rest so you don't have a relapse. *You're* the one who wants to work."

". . . and I've got to study really hard if I want to get my high-school equivalency diploma," Holly barreled on, ignoring her sister. "And I've got to see Dr. Frazier in Burlington once a week . . ."

June just stared at Holly, her lips pressed together. "That's what it really is, isn't it?" she whispered.

"What?" Holly asked, confused.

"You still think you're going to die," June said, "so you're afraid to love somebody." Tears started to rim her lower lashes.

Holly hung her head.

June grabbed Holly's arm and shook it gently. "You're *not* going to die!" she said fiercely. "You're my big sister and we're gonna be best friends 'til we're old and decrepit and our teeth are falling out. We're gonna outlive everybody, even our husbands, and then we'll get a house together and live there 'til we're ninety-five. Maybe older!"

Holly laughed. "Sounds good," she said, trying to imagine herself stooped and toothless. It wasn't a pretty picture, but it sure beat the alternative. "I just don't want things to get messy," she insisted. "I mean, even if I did go out with Chris, it couldn't last past the summer, anyway. He's going to Yale in the fall. I have to be practical about this."

"No you don't," June said firmly. "Stop being so responsible all the time!"

Holly smiled. "But I'm a Paige!"

June rolled her eyes. "I know, I know. A Paige is always responsible and always on time. But forget all that. It's time to let go."

The young man with the clipboard entered

the room again, followed by Sal and Annie, who galloped over to their older sisters.

"How'd it go?" Holly asked them.

"Great!" Annie enthused. "They took about a dozen pictures of us . . ."

". . . posing with *two* bikes," Sal continued. "If we win, maybe we'll each get one!"

"And the photographer said we were very cooperative," Annie said. "He said it was a pleasure working with us."

"So what happens now?" June asked.

"Jay looks at all the pictures and makes a decision in a week or two," Sal said.

"He'd better decide on us," Annie said. "Did you see those bikes? They were unbelievable! Indexing shifting, twenty-one speeds . . ."

". . . gel seat, carbon fiber frame," Sal continued as the twins headed for the screen door. Holly and June started after them.

"Don't forget what I said," June whispered in Holly's ear. "Do what makes you feel good. Live!"

"Cynthia Dansby," the young man with the clipboard called out as Holly pushed open the screen door.

Chapter Ten

"But is the movie supposed to be any good?" Holly asked June after dinner Tuesday evening. Holly stood at the shared dresser in their bedroom, looking in the mirror as she brushed her black hair. It hung forward over her shoulders, long and thick. June stood beside her, carefully applying mascara.

"Who cares if it's any good," June said. "It's the only movie in town, it's relatively recent, and what else is there to do tonight?"

June had a point. Except for what was going on at The Mountain, there wasn't much nightlife in Landon. "What's it called?" Holly asked, drawing the brush through her hair again.

"*Love on the Run,*" June said. "I'm not sure

what it's about, but with a title like that, it's got to be romantic."

"I guess." Holly put down the hairbrush with the sterling-silver handle she'd inherited from her grandmother. Then she noticed something about the brush and picked it up again. "Oh, no, this can't be happening," she moaned.

"What is it?" June asked.

Holly showed her sister the hairbrush. It was completely filled with strands of her black hair.

"So?" June said.

"Look how much hair is in it," Holly said. "Much more than usual. My hair's falling out."

June scoffed. "Of course it isn't! You should see my brush." June opened the top drawer of her side of the dresser and started fishing around in the clutter. "That is, if I could find it."

Holly pulled a large handful of hair from her hairbrush. Hair loss was one of the warning signs of lupus. She'd never had it before, but she'd read about it in the brochures Dr. Frazier had given her. "I bet it means I'm having a relapse," Holly worried. "I know I should be prepared for this . . . prepared to—to die . . . but I stupidly thought I might be getting better. What a joke!"

"Stop talking like that. You are getting better," June cried. "Here!" June triumphantly pulled her wooden-handled hairbrush out of her messy drawer. The brush was loaded with her fine light brown hair. "See? Mine's the same as yours."

"But you don't clean yours every day the way I do," Holly pointed out. "That could be weeks' worth."

"Look, Holly," June said. "I know you think this means something dire. I've read those lupus brochures, too. But you're being paranoid. Dr. Frazier just checked you out yesterday and said you were fine."

"I guess . . ." Holly said, throwing the hair in the straw trash basket next to her bed.

"And hair loss goes in cycles," June added. "You tend to lose more in the summer 'cause that's when your hair grows more."

"Where'd you hear that?" Holly asked.

June shrugged. "I read an article. So let's not worry any more about it, okay? Let's just worry about having a good time tonight."

Holly gave June a kiss on her plump cheek.

"What was that for?" June asked.

Holly smiled at her sister. "For being my

best friend," she said. "You always know how to make me feel better."

The theater lobby was jammed with people, mostly teenagers like Holly and June. It was easy to tell the locals from guests of The Mountain. The locals, like Holly, wore faded jeans, T-shirts, denim jackets. The outsiders, though many also wore jeans, looked like they were *trying* to look casual. Their expensive polo shirts were purposely untucked, their shoes and sneakers purposely untied.

There was a snack bar toward the back of the dark wood-paneled lobby. Faded red velvet ropes fenced in a line of people waiting to buy candy and popcorn.

"You want anything?" Holly asked her sister.

"Oooh! Yeah!" June said. "How 'bout a large . . ." June's mouth suddenly dropped open. "Uh-oh." She was staring at something over Holly's shoulder.

"What?" Holly asked, turning around to look.

"No! Don't!" June pleaded, ducking her head and putting a hand up to shield her face. "Don't look. You'll just call attention to us."

"June!" Holly said, grabbing her sister by the shoulders. "What's wrong?"

"Brett's here!" June hissed. "With Chris." June's brown eyes were wide with fear.

"So?" Holly asked. "What's wrong with that? I thought everything was going so well."

"With *Lucia*," June said. "Lucia Chatsworth with the red hair. But I can't let him see me this way. He might recognize me and realize I've been lying to him. It will ruin everything!"

"So what do you want to do?" Holly asked. "Do you want to go home?"

June pursed her full lips as she considered their dilemma. "We already bought the tickets," she said. "Let's just go in real quick and hope they don't see us."

"Holly!"

Holly felt a hand on her shoulder. She didn't even have to turn around to know it was the same hand that had touched her this morning. It sent the same waves of heat and excitement through her.

"Chris!" she exclaimed, turning around.

"I'll find us a seat," June whispered into the back of Holly's head. "Look for me inside."

Holly smiled up at Chris and felt like she was swimming in the swirling blue of his eyes. He smiled back at her warmly.

"How are you feeling?" he asked with concern. "You get home okay?"

"You bet," Holly assured him. "Thanks for asking. And how was the rest of your private lesson with Mrs. Faulkner? Or should I say . . . Jill?"

Chris laughed, embarrassed. "You caught that part, huh? She's harmless, though. I never take her seriously."

"Sounds like she takes *you* pretty seriously," Holly said. "And she's not bad looking, for an older woman."

"Sounds like you're jealous!" Chris teased.

Holly blushed. She hadn't even thought about it before, but maybe Chris was right.

"Don't worry," Chris said. "Even if Jill . . . uh, Mrs. Faulkner, was sixteen and single, you wouldn't have to worry. She's no competition for you."

Now Holly was really embarrassed. Though she'd been flirting with Chris, she hadn't expected him to respond so . . . obviously. He was practically saying she was the girl he was interested in.

"Yo, Chris, what's up?" Brett asked, appearing by Chris's side. "I thought you were getting candy." Brett's expression darkened when he saw Holly. "Hey, isn't this the waitress from the diner?" The way he said "waitress" it sounded more like *worm*.

"This is Holly Paige," Chris said, lightly touching Holly's shoulder.

Holly felt like he was protecting her from Brett's snobbery. Not that she needed his help. She could think of any number of snappy comebacks to put Brett in his place. But remembering how much June and Chris liked him, she kept her mouth shut. What did those two see in this guy, anyway? Whatever it was, it was invisible to Holly.

"So, who're you here with?" Chris asked Holly. "You want to sit with us?"

Holly bit her lip, trying to figure out how to answer. She really did want to sit with Chris, but she couldn't tell him she was here with her sister. Then Chris would invite June to sit with them, too, and that would blow June's cover. "Uh . . . no one," she fibbed.

"Then you *have* to sit with us, right, Brett?" Chris asked, shooting Brett a warning look.

Brett shrugged. "Sure," he said. "I'll get us something to eat. What would you like, Holly?"

Holly appreciated that Brett was now trying to be polite, but she didn't want to owe him anything. "Nothing, thank you," she said.

"We'll meet you inside," Chris said, placing his hand on Holly's back and guiding her toward the double doors. The warmth of his touch made Holly tingle. She didn't want to break away, but she had to talk to June.

"Can I meet you inside, too?" she asked. "I need to use the ladies' room."

"Sure," Chris said, going in. "I'll flag you down."

Holly waited a minute, then followed a group of friends into the auditorium and started scanning the seats for her sister. She spotted June slumped low in a seat on the far right near the back. "June!" Holly hissed, sidling through the empty aisle.

June looked up fearfully, then smiled when she recognized her sister. "What happened?" she asked.

"He wants me to sit with them," Holly said guiltily. "But I'll tell him I can't. I don't want to leave you alone."

"That's ridiculous!" June retorted. "Why would you want to sit with me when you can sit with a cute, rich, adorable guy?"

"'Cause I'm not going to bail out on my sister just because a guy comes along," Holly said. "Besides, I made plans with you first."

"I'll be fine," June insisted. "I *want* you to sit with Chris."

"You sure?" Holly asked.

June pushed Holly toward the aisle. "Go!" she said. "I'll meet you by the car after the movie."

Holly found Chris sitting by himself in a center seat near the front.

"Hi," he said softly as she sat down next to him.

"Hi," she answered shyly.

"We keep bumping into each other," Chris said. "Three times in the past two days. It must be fate." His gaze held hers with such intensity that Holly couldn't turn away. He smelled faintly of shampoo and after-shave. Holly breathed in his scent and smiled.

"Hey, guys," Brett said, breaking the spell as he came down the aisle on Chris's side. His arms were loaded with popcorn, soda, and candy. "Here," he said to Holly, holding out a paper cup, "diet Coke. I figured I couldn't go wrong. All girls drink diet soda."

"Thanks," Holly said, taking the cold cup. A straw poked through the translucent plastic top. Brett handed Chris a gigantic tub of pop-

corn and sat down next to Chris with a foot-
long chocolate candy bar. While Holly still didn't
like Brett, she had to admit he could be decent
when he wanted to be.

The lights started to dim. Holly looked back
toward June. At the same moment, June
caught her eye and gave her a thumbs-up. The
movie started, and Holly quickly became
caught up in the drama of two teenaged outlaws, a boy and a girl, on the run as they
robbed convenience stores and gas stations. It
was dumb, of course, but exciting and romantic since of course the teenagers were madly in
love. They'd steal kisses, and more, at odd moments like when they were hiding in their con-
vertible under a bridge while the police cars,
sirens wailing, shot past overhead.

Holly couldn't help picturing herself in that
car under the bridge, with Chris's arms around
her. Her heart beat faster as the girl and guy
melted into a long, lingering, passionate kiss.
Then she became aware of the fact that her
arm shared an armrest with Chris's arm and
that their pulses were pounding to the same
beat. Could Chris be thinking what she was
thinking?

As if he'd read her mind, Chris reached for

her hand and wrapped his fingers around hers. Holly's heart beat even faster. She knew she should resist, should remember all the reasons she'd given June why this could never work out. But the delicious feeling of Chris's lean body beneath the thin fabric of his shirt washed all her reason away. June had said she should do what made her feel good, and this definitely felt good.

As the movie neared the end, the police closed in on the outlaw couple culminating in a big shoot-out in a Western ghost town. The girl, hiding inside an empty cobweb-filled saloon, took a bullet in the chest and collapsed in her lover's arms.

Holly drew in a breath. She didn't like the way this movie was going. Would that be her and Chris at some point in the future? Would she, like the dying girl on the screen, pour out her love for him as the blood poured from her body?

Holly closed her eyes and shifted closer to Chris, unable to watch the rest. She tried to comfort herself with his warmth, his solidness, his deep, regular breathing. She tried to remind herself that this wasn't a movie. She was alive and well, more or less, and not some outlaw on the run. So why did she feel this stitch in her chest? Why was she having so much trouble breathing?

As the credits rolled, Chris let go of her hand. "Pretty intense romance," he said in her ear.

Holly nodded as she turned to look at him. His eyes glowed in the reflected light of the movie screen. His face was just inches from hers, his lips were slightly parted. Holly was aching to kiss him, as the outlaw girl had kissed her lover right before she died. And she felt Chris wanted it as badly as she did. But they weren't even on a date. Still, Chris moved a little closer. Holly didn't back away.

The lights came up suddenly and, all around them, people were standing up, putting on jackets, and chattering about the movie. Holly leaned back in her seat and took a deep breath. The mood was broken. Anyway, it was bad enough she was out in public with a Franklin. She didn't want some nosy neighbor reporting back to her parents that she had been seen *kissing* one.

Holly stood up quickly. "I'd better go."

"Wait!" Chris said, standing, too. "When do I get to see you again? We can't keep leaving it up to fate. Let's go out on a real date."

Holly hesitated. She wanted to say yes, but all those reasons were coming back to her now—her parents, her responsibilities, her illness, and the fact that they were totally wrong for each other. It was one thing to get swept away while his arms were around her, but the movie was over and it was time to get back to reality.

"I don't know . . ." Holly said. "Thanks for asking, but . . ."

"Look," Chris said, taking her hand. "At least don't say no. You don't have to say yes, either. Just say you'll think about it."

His hands were strong, and his eyes were pleading. She could always say no later. "All right," Holly agreed. "I'll think about it."

Chapter Eleven

"Wake up, sleepyhead!"

Chris, his eyes still glued shut, groaned as he heard his mother's voice and felt her gentle hand on the top of his head. His dream had just been getting to the good part. He and Holly had been in his Jeep, speeding down a desert highway. In his dream, Holly, dressed all in black with sunglasses and a straw hat, was a spy. He was helping her escape from FBI agents who happened to be driving his father's Bentley as they pursued them. Holly had just wrapped her arms around Chris's neck and was starting to whisper that she'd go out with him when Chris had felt his mother's hand.

"What?" Chris moaned, rubbing the sleep from his eyes and opening them a crack.

His mother, dressed as usual in linen pants, a silk blouse, and brown loafers, sat at the edge of his bed with a piece of paper in her hand. Her blond hair was pulled back in a simple ponytail, and her tan face was deeply lined on the forehead and around the mouth. "I want to go over the guest list," his mother said.

"What guest list?" Chris asked, confused. He was still thinking about Holly and the Jeep.

"For your birthday party," his mother said. "Remember? You're turning eighteen next week."

Chris sat up and leaned against the plump down pillows. No wonder he'd forgotten. He'd blocked it out. His parents had planned this thing like it was the major social event of the century. They were inviting every important person they knew, with an emphasis on lawyers, judges, and people in politics. It was less a birthday party than a convention of people who might help advance Chris's career as future president of the United States.

"Invite whoever you want," Chris said. "It's *your* party."

Chris's mother looked hurt. "Chris, we're doing this for you. We want you to invite your friends and have a good time."

"Oh, yeah?" Chris asked. "Well, when will I have a chance to talk to them? I'll be busy networking the whole time."

"That's not fair," his mother said. "There's nothing wrong with meeting people who might be helpful to you later on. That's how most business gets done—through personal connections. But let's not worry about that now. Let's talk about who *you* want to invite."

"I thought I gave you a list already," Chris said.

"Yes," his mother answered, "but you haven't invited a date yet."

So that was it. Not only did his parents want to program this whole party, they wanted to pick his date, too. Chris knew from experience that his mother wasn't here to ask him who he wanted to invite. If he just waited a few more seconds, she'd be telling him who *she* had in mind.

"You know, Chris," his mother said, "if you can't think of anyone, your father and I were thinking you might want to ask Hilary Durham. She's a lovely girl. It was so nice to dine with her and her parents the other night. I didn't know she had gotten into Harvard."

Chris almost exploded with laughter. Why

hadn't he been able to predict this, too? It was so obvious. His parents had been pushing Hilary on him practically his whole life.

"I don't know," Chris said. "I need to think about it."

"What's to think about?" his mother asked. "There's no one else, is there?"

Chris thought again of how good it had felt last night to have Holly snuggled against him, her silky hair brushing against his neck. He thought how close they'd come to kissing if only the lights hadn't come up when they did. Then he thought, again, how Holly would look by his side at his birthday party, and how his parents would look at her. He pictured her in a black dress and pearls, like all the other women wore to these things. Come to think of it, she looked pretty good in his imagination. Maybe he *could* invite her.

But it didn't come down to just what she looked like. As soon as he mentioned her name, his mother would start grilling him about Holly's pedigree. And as soon as his mother heard words like diner and waitress, her eyes would glaze over and her ears would go deaf. There was no point even bringing it up.

"I don't know," Chris said. "I'll have to get back to you."

"Well, don't wait too long," his mother said. "If you're going to invite Hilary, it would be rude not to let her know as soon as possible."

"Ooooh, Brett, that feels so good," June sighed Wednesday afternoon as she felt his hands spread suntan lotion all over her back. She lay on a chaise lounge, on her stomach, by the waterfall that crashed splashily into the pool below.

"Not half as good as I feel," Brett said in a husky voice. His hands roamed lower, slipping down to her legs and rubbing the backs of her thighs.

June reached up to the table beside her and took her BLT off the plate. Taking a big bite, she put the sandwich back and chewed with her eyes closed. So what if she'd had to slink around the movie theater last night like the two outlaws in the movie? So what if Brett didn't know her real name or even her real hair color? What they had right now was plenty real, and she had their date tonight to look forward to. As far as June was concerned, life was just perfect.

"I'm glad you don't have to run away again," Brett said, "'cause I was thinking . . . my mom's going to be out sailing all day on Mansfield Lake, and you haven't seen our suite. Maybe you'd like to come up for a visit."

June smiled lazily. She'd seen Brett's suite twice already, though he didn't know it. And she'd be cleaning it again in just a few . . . June sat up abruptly. "What time is it?" she asked, panicking.

Brett checked his watch. "Five after one. Don't tell me you have to . . ."

June leaped off the lounge chair and grabbed her knapsack. "Sorry," she said, jamming her feet into her rubber flip-flops. "I'll meet you tonight, okay? Main Dining Room, eight o'clock."

"Lucia!" Brett called after her, but June couldn't stop, not even for him. Mrs. Donnely had already warned her what would happen if she showed up late again. June could kiss her job good-bye. And how was it going to look when she showed up at Housekeeping smelling of coconut oil? Flip-flops flapping, June raced across the hot pavement.

"Chris? Is that you? I can't believe it! How are you?"

It had been months since Chris had heard his sister's voice. Since their father had cut Blaire off, Chris had found it harder to stay in touch. At school he'd been able to call long distance to San Francisco without his father knowing. Since he'd come back home, though, there was no way to place a call from home without leaving a record on the phone bill. That's why Chris had applied for his own long-distance calling card. It had just come in the mail today.

"I'm good," Chris said, locking his bedroom door and walking with the cordless phone to the high-backed green leather armchair by the window. Chris hated the stuffy old armchair, but it had been in his family for generations and his mom had insisted he keep it in his room. He dropped down into the armchair and propped his feet up on a matching green leather ottoman. "How's the band?"

"We're cookin'," Blaire said. "We'd been playing some little coffeehouses and neighborhood joints, but we just got a great gig. We're going on tour to open for the X-Citements!"

"No kidding?" Chris asked. "That's great! Uh . . . who are the X-Citements?"

"Whoa, Chris, you must have been pretty

out of it at Dover. They're this hot new Seattle
post-grunge band and they're just taking off.
And hopefully we'll follow right behind them."

"I'm sure you will," he said wistfully. He got
out of his chair and knelt on the window seat
overlooking the grounds of his parents' vast es-
tate. Chris's bedroom window faced the back
of their twenty-room mansion, and the formal
garden below covered nearly an acre. Sculpted
bushes formed a square border, fencing in clas-
sical statues and rosebushes of every shade.

Chris's mother was down there, giving instructions to the gardener about the lush rosebushes. She was fanatical that the grounds be
maintained as a showpiece of her talent—
even if others did the down-on-hands-and-
knees work for her. She rarely left the
property except to attend social events at The
Mountain. Blaire had always said that was why
she wanted to get as far away from home as
she could. She couldn't stand her mother's
limited life, and their parents' limited ways of
thinking. The question was—was Chris brave
enough to follow?

"What's the matter, Chris Cross?" Blaire
asked, using the name she'd made up for him
when they were little. "You sound sad."

"Huh?" Chris asked. "No, not sad exactly. Just confused, I guess."

"Talk to me," Blaire said. "Dad still getting on your nerves?"

"Of course," Chris said, "but that's not it. It's about my birthday party."

"Hint, hint," Blaire joked. "Don't worry, I won't forget to buy you a present."

Chris laughed. "Yeah, send me another can of tennis balls like you did last year. I keep losin' 'em."

"Your eighteenth birthday," Blaire mused. "The day your trust fund matures. You should have quite a bundle in your name now that Mom and Dad have disinherited me. I wish I'd waited 'til I turned eighteen so I wouldn't have to wait tables today. Take the money and run, right?"

"You need money?" Chris asked. "I can send you some. I've got almost five thousand in my personal account. Dad doesn't know how I spend it."

"No, thanks," Blaire said. "With this gig we've got coming up, I should be just fine. But getting back to your birthday, what's the problem?" Blaire asked. "Does it have something to do with a girl?"

"Yeah . . ." Chris said glumly, toying with the dangling string that hung from the window shade.

"Do you like her?"

"Yeah."

"Does she like you?"

"I think so."

"So what's the problem?"

Chris yanked on the string, and the shade dropped down, blocking his view of the garden and his mother. "I want to invite her to my birthday party," he said, "but I don't think she'll get the parental seal of approval."

"What's the matter with her?" Blaire asked. "Her father not a senator, governor, or member of the Cabinet?"

Chris laughed. "Actually, he *was* in politics. He was mayor of Landon ten years ago."

"Tom Paige?" Blaire asked. "The carpenter?"

"Good memory," Chris said.

"I think I also remember a chubby little brother who had a major crush on the mayor's daughter in sixth grade. Am I right or am I right? What was her name again?"

"Holly," Chris said.

"Whoa . . ." Blaire said, her tone becoming serious. "I just remembered something else. Holly's father fought our dad about The Mountain to the bitter end. Dad still blames him for all the extra taxes he has to pay. And we never passed Mr. Paige in town without him looking like he wanted to stick a knife in Dad's back. Yup, Chris, I see what you mean. You are asking for trouble."

Chris paced across the navy-and-maroon antique rug to the door of his room. "So what are you saying?" he asked. "That I should just forget about it?"

"Of course not!" Blaire said. "What do you care what Dad or Mom thinks? If you want something, go for it! That's what I would do."

At the door, Chris turned and paced back toward the window. "Yeah," he said, "but that's the difference between you and me. You're not afraid of them. I am." He turned again and headed back for the door.

"They're not going to disinherit you for inviting Holly to your party," Blaire said. "Of course, they may not speak to you for a few weeks, but that might not be so bad."

Chris laughed. "Guess you're right. I want to ask her. And so I will."

"Good."

Chris stopped by the door, leaned against it, and sighed. "Now the only problem is getting Holly to say yes."

*   *   *

Mrs. Donnely wasn't in the basement office when June arrived, breathless, from the pool. Maybe this was a good sign. Maybe the head housekeeper was upstairs somewhere, supervising one of the other maids. If June could only get up to the third floor and get her cart out of the closet without being seen, she'd be home free. Even if she did run into Mrs. Donnely up there, Mrs. Donnely wouldn't know exactly what time she'd started work.

June raced out of the Housekeeping office toward the elevator and jammed her finger against the button. It was a quarter after one. She looked up and down the concrete hallway, fearing to see a tall, gangly woman in a cream-colored uniform. The only person she saw was a maintenance worker in a green jumpsuit, pushing a trolley loaded with trash bags.

Where was that elevator? June banged on the button again. Why was it whenever you were in a hurry, things seemed to take longer? The gray doors opened onto a redwood paneled elevator with brass trim. June jumped on, pressed three, and jiggled nervously.

Oh, please don't let her see me, June begged silently. *I promise I'll never be late again. I'll hang an alarm clock around my neck, I'll dust every room twice, I'll . . .*

The elevator doors opened onto cream-colored walls and rose-bordered carpeting. June poked her head out and peered down the hall. There were a few maid's carts parked way down at the other end of the hall, but no sign of Mrs. Donnely. June darted out of the elevator and made a dash for the maid's closet. There was her cart, exactly as she'd left it, stacked with towels and cleaning supplies. Now all June had to do was get the cart inside her first suite and Mrs. Donnely would never know the difference.

Pulling the heavy cart toward the door, June made her way into the hallway. Suite 324 was first on her list. The one right next to Brett's suite. Reaching into the pocket of her uniform, June pulled out her electronic card. Another fifteen seconds and she'd be safely inside.

"What do you think you're doing?"

June turned around and found herself face to bony face with Mrs. Donnely. There was nothing but cool malice in the head house-keeper's gray eyes.

"Uh . . ." June tried to think up a reasonable-sounding excuse. After all, she was already on the hall with her cart. She could lie and say she'd done another room first, then go back and clean that room later. But what if Mrs. Donnely didn't believe her and went to check that room? Mrs. Donnely would catch her in the lie and June would lose her job anyway.

"June, this is the third time in three days that you've been late," Mrs. Donnely warned. "Did I or did I not make it very clear the last time what would happen if you were late again?"

June hung her head. She could feel it coming. There was no use trying to fight it now. "You made it clear," she said softly.

"I'm sorry, June," Mrs. Donnely said, "but we cannot tolerate such unprofessional behavior. I'm afraid I'll have to . . ."

"June!" a male voice called from a few yards away. "I'm glad I found you."

June looked up with surprise. Who was calling her? No one besides Mrs. Donnely knew her at the hotel. No one except . . .

June gasped in horror as she saw the tall, young man with glossy black hair pad barefoot down the hall in his baggy blue shorts and Dover Prep T-shirt. He was staring right at her, and he was smiling. It was Brett!

Chapter Twelve

June wanted to dive into the bin of dirty towels and hide. This had to be the worst moment of her life. Not only was she about to lose her job, she was also going to lose her big chance to find romance *and* get out of this flea-bitten little town. There was no way Brett would ever talk to her again now that he'd seen through her disguise. Feeling the tears well in her eyes, June hung her head so neither Brett nor Mrs. Donnely could see.

"June," Brett said again, coming closer. "I just wanted to thank you."

June raised her eyes wonderingly. Mrs. Donnely, too, looked at Brett in confusion.

"You did such a great job cleaning our suite just now," Brett continued, stopping in front of them. "I know it took you longer than usual, and that was my fault." He turned to Mrs. Donnely. "Are you June's boss?"

"I'm the head housekeeper," Mrs. Donnely said proudly. "And you are?"

"My mom and I are guests of the hotel," Brett said. "*And* friends of the Franklins."

Mrs. Donnely's proud expression was replaced by a friendlier one. "Oh, really?"

"Yes," Brett said, "and I just wanted to compliment you on your housekeeping staff. This young lady has really gone above and beyond the call of duty in making us feel *welcome* here." Brett winked at June. If June hadn't been so nervous and upset, she might even have laughed.

Mrs. Donnely turned to June. "You mean you cleaned 322 *before* 324? That's why you're late getting started here?"

June nodded mutely. Her head was spinning from how quickly this situation was turning around.

Mrs. Donnely sniffed. "Well, you should have consulted me first before changing the schedule, but as long as our guests are satisfied, I suppose that's all right." Without another word, Mrs. Donnely headed down the hall toward the elevator.

June waited until the doors had closed behind the housekeeper before daring to speak to Brett, who waited by her side.

"How did you know it was me?" she asked finally.

"I figured something was up when you kept running away at exactly one o'clock, so I followed you."

"You must think I'm a total jerk," June said. "And I guess I am. I lied about so many things, I tried to make you believe I was someone I wasn't . . ."

"June . . ." Brett tried to cut in, but she couldn't stop the words from pouring out.

". . . and I don't deserve the way you stood up for me just now. You should have told Mrs. Donnely I tried to pass myself off as a guest. That would have been grounds for firing me even if I hadn't been late, which I was . . ."

"June . . ."

"Oh, boy," June went on, "my life is really a mess, though at least I still have my job, thanks to you. But I totally understand that you'll want to cancel our date tonight."

"June!" Brett exclaimed. "Will you please let me say something?"

June was startled into silence.

Brett looked up and down the hall to make

sure no one was around, then he placed his hands on her shoulders. "I don't care what your name is," he said, drawing her closer. "June, Lucia, what's the difference? The important thing is, you're a really hot girl and we've been having fun together."

"Really?" June asked, unable to believe her luck. Not only would she get to keep her job, it looked like Brett was going to stick around, too.

"Really," Brett said, letting his lips touch hers ever so softly.

June's body melted against his as she returned his kiss. Then she remembered where she was and pulled back. If socializing with guests was forbidden, kissing them in public hallways had to be. "Sorry," she whispered. "I don't want to get in any more trouble."

"I understand," he said, gazing at her with a sexy smile. "But we can pick up again later where we left off."

The way Brett was looking at her sent tingles through June's entire body. She'd never gone further than kissing a guy, but she had a feeling things could go a *lot* further with Brett, if she let him.

"So?" June said. "Are we still meeting at eight o'clock, Main Dining Room?"

Brett looked thoughtful. "Well, actually," he said, "there's been a slight change of plan. I've got to have an early dinner tonight in Burlington with my mom and some family friends. I told my mom I had plans, of course, but this is something I just can't get out of."

"Oh," June whispered, her spirits sinking.

"But I wouldn't break our date for anything," Brett reassured her. "So why don't we meet *after* dinner?"

Well, it wasn't the Main Dining Room, but it was still a date with Brett. "Where?" June asked.

"You know where the golf clubhouse is?" Brett asked. "Past the pool and the tennis courts?"

"Yes," June said, "but doesn't the golf course close at seven?"

Brett laughed. "We're not going golfing!" He drew her toward him again. "Oh, no. I've got other plans for you and me. We'll go for a walk . . . a moonlit romantic stroll. What do you say? Nine o'clock? How does that sound?"

June smiled, thinking again of their kiss. "It sounds great!" she said.

"Let's see, what looks good today?" Joe Crocker, a bank clerk from Landon Savings &

Loan down the street, studied the diner menu
as he always did—like it was a sacred document
containing all the secrets of the universe.
"Hmmm . . ." he pondered. "Maybe I'll have
grilled ham and Swiss on rye and a side of
fries."

Holly, standing behind the counter of Peg's,
didn't write down anything on her order pad.
She'd been through this before.

". . . or maybe I'll have the Wednesday tur-
key special." Joe looked up from the menu
with a worried frown on his fleshy face. "Does
that come with mashed potatoes?"

"And gravy," Holly said patiently.

Joe looked back at the menu. "I don't know.
Tuna on whole wheat sounds pretty good." He
scratched at the few wispy hairs remaining on
his bald head.

"You want more time to decide?" Holly
asked. "I could come back." Saying this always
did the trick with Joe.

"No!" he said, panicking. "I'll decide . . .
uh . . . let's see. He took one more quick look
at the menu, then snapped it shut. "Make it a
hamburger," he said. "Well done."

"You got it," Holly said, finally writing something down. Though Joe probably didn't real-

ize it, he ordered the same thing every day, just like everybody else. The only difference was he took a lot longer to make up his mind.

Holly ripped the order off her pad and clipped it to the kitchen window. "Burger well!" she shouted at her mother, who stood by the grill.

Her mother took another raw patty off the pile and threw it onto the sizzling counter. "How you doing out there, Hol?" she asked, approaching the window. "You need a break?"

Holly's feet were hurting from being on them nonstop since eight this morning, and her wrists ached from carrying all those heavy plates. But she couldn't leave her mother in the lurch. There was only one other waitress on duty, and the lunch hour was almost over. Things would slow down soon.

"I'm fine," she said with a cheerful smile.

Her mother smiled back, the worry momentarily lifting from her green eyes. Holly knew that no matter how long she stayed in remission, her mother would never stop dwelling on her illness. At night sometimes, when Holly was drifting off to sleep, she'd see her mother open the bedroom door and look in on her, probably to make sure she was still breathing. Holly felt terrible that she'd caused her mother so much anxiety, so she tried to do everything she could to bring life back to normal.

The front door of the diner opened again, and Chris walked in by himself. Unlike the last time he'd come in, when he'd been wearing his sweaty tennis clothes, this time he looked almost dressed up. He wore neatly pressed chinos, an olive-and-gray button-down shirt, and shiny penny loafers. His thick blond hair looked recently trimmed. Holly wondered if maybe, just maybe, Chris had dressed that way because he wanted to look nice for her.

Holly came around the counter and approached him. "This is the fourth time in three days," she joked. "Is it still fate?"

From the way Chris smiled down at her, Holly knew the answer. "You got a minute?" he asked. "I mean, I don't want to keep you from your work. I'll order something."

"Sure," Holly said, grabbing a menu from a stack by the cash register. "Sit anywhere you like."

Chris slid into a booth in the back by the jukebox, and Holly handed him a menu. He took it but didn't open it. "I don't want to pressure you to go out with me," he said, his blue eyes earnest. "Take as long as you want to make up your mind. But I wanted to give you something else to think about."

Holly put her order pad in her apron pocket and waited.

Chris took a deep breath and exhaled sharply. "My birthday's coming up," he said, "and my parents are throwing me this big bash Saturday night at the hotel. I'd like you to be my date."

Holly stared at Chris, stunned. After all the talks she'd had with June about Brett, this was the last thing she'd ever expected to hear. Even if boys like Chris dated townie girls like her, they didn't invite them to society functions. They didn't parade them in front of their friends and family as if they were actually *serious* about them. And what about all the trouble between Chris's family and her own? Chris didn't believe this date was something that could actually happen, did he?

"It's nice of you to offer," she began, but Chris cut her off.

"I know what you're thinking," he said. "I know all the arguments why it would never work. *But I don't care!* I want to get to know you, Holly. If anyone has a problem with that, it's their problem. And if you want to be with me, you shouldn't let anyone else tell you not to. It's *your* life, Holly, and mine. We're the ones who should decide."

Holly sank down into the seat across from Chris, and for a moment, all she could do was stare at him. Every word he'd said was true. And she *did* want to go out with him. But how could she ever tell her parents what she was up to? They'd never forgive her.

"What do you say, Holly?" Chris asked, leaning across the table to take her hand. Holly glanced nervously toward the kitchen to see if her mother was looking, but Peg Paige was out of sight.

Holly stared into Chris's eyes and felt herself weakening. Never in her life had a boy spoken to her this way. Never before had she felt so strongly attracted to anyone. And who knew how much time she had? Was she going to throw away what could be her only chance for happiness? And how could she say no to him when he was willing to risk so much?

Holly squeezed Chris's hand. "I'd love to go, Chris," she said.

Chris's face lit up. "Really?"

"Really."

Chris hopped up out of his seat. "Then we should celebrate," he said.

"What do you mean?" Holly asked, also standing. Her mother could peek out the window at any minute. Holly didn't want her to guess what was going on.

"My party's not 'til Saturday," Chris said. "I can't wait that long to see you again. How 'bout right now? I want to talk to you, find out all about you. I feel like I've waited my whole life for this, and I can't wait any longer!"

Holly laughed. "I wish I'd known you felt this way in sixth grade. Maybe then I wouldn't have been so mean to you!" Holly glanced around the diner. It was still half-full with customers, but the crowd was thinning out. "Tell you what," she told Chris. "Give me half an hour to finish up here, then I can meet you somewhere."

"We could go bike riding," Chris said. "I've got a couple bikes over at my parents' house."

Holly bit her lip. Dr. Frazier had said she couldn't overexert herself, and riding a bike was probably pushing it. "How 'bout we go for a walk?" she suggested.

"Anything," Chris said. "I'll meet you outside at two o'clock."

Chapter Thirteen

Holly was trying her best to keep up with Chris's brisk pace. *But a recovering invalid's no match for a professional tennis instructor,* she thought wryly as she stepped over tree roots and rocks embedded in the hard-packed earth. Her legs felt heavy and weak, and she was finding it a little tough to breathe.

"You okay?" Chris asked, turning back to look at her.

Holly nodded and leaned against a tree for support. "I'm fine," she said, trying to catch her breath. "Just out of shape, like I said."

"Well, maybe we should find a place to sit down." Chris pointed to a grassy knoll overlooking the valley. Clumps of buttercups, daisies, and violets were scattered over the sun-soaked hill. "How 'bout there?" he asked. "We could spread our blanket and have a snack." Chris had returned from the hotel with a big picnic basket and a giant blanket with The Mountain's logo stamped on it.

Holly was torn. It would feel so lovely to sit in the sun and smell the flowers. But she didn't want to get another rash. "How about over there?" she suggested, pointing to a shady spot beneath some cedar trees.

"Still on the lam, huh?" Chris joked, heading for the trees.

"What's that supposed to mean?" Holly asked, trudging behind him.

Chris stopped walking and turned around. "The hat, the sunglasses, hanging out in dark places. You must be hiding *something*." He was smiling, but there was a seriousness in his eyes.

Holly panicked. While she was sure Chris didn't know about her illness, he definitely knew something was up. How long could she keep hiding the truth from him?

"I just don't like the sun, okay?" she snapped.

Chris was instantly apologetic. "Sure," he said. "You just want to keep your skin young and beautiful, right? So you'll never get wrinkles."

I might never live long enough to get wrinkles even if I do sit in the sun, Holly thought. She felt bad, too, for reacting so sharply to Chris's joke. "I'm sorry," she said. "I'm just a little tired, that's all."

Chris put his arm around her and led her to the shade beneath the trees. There, he spread the blanket and began unpacking the picnic basket. There was a giant bottle of mineral water, crystal goblets, a long skinny loaf of French bread, a round of Brie cheese, and a mesh bag filled with apples, oranges, and grapes.

"Wow!" Holly exclaimed, sinking down onto the blanket over its cushion of thick grass. "You didn't have to do this!"

"I wanted to," Chris said, taking two white linen napkins out of the basket and handing one to Holly. The napkins, too, had The Mountain's logo embroidered in gold thread. Chris poured some sparkling water into a goblet and handed it to Holly. After he'd poured some for himself, he held up his goblet. "To us," he said. "To breaking the rules."

"But not the glass," Holly joked as her goblet clinked against Chris's. "It's too beautiful."

"I nabbed all this stuff out of the Main Dining Room," Chris explained.

Holly exploded into laughter.

"What's so funny?" he asked.

Holly was laughing so hard, she could barely find the breath to speak. "You know that saying—if the mountain won't go to Mohammed? Well, here my parents have been telling me my whole life to stay away from The Mountain. Now you're bringing The Mountain to me!"

Chris laughed, too. "It just proves my point," he said. "We can overcome anything— even our parents' stupid narrow-mindedness— if we stick together and don't back down. Why should they run our lives? We're practically adults. We can make our own decisions."

Chris's usually gentle expression was transformed by his words. A flush of red had risen to his cheeks, his eyes were ablaze, and his jaw was set into a hard, firm line. It occurred to Holly that there was a lot beneath Chris's words that she didn't understand.

"Tell me about your parents," Holly said. "How are they trying to run your life?"

Chris leaned back on the blanket, propping himself on one elbow, and stared across the valley at another tree-covered mountain. "I've been programmed from birth," he said bitterly.

"For politics. My father's convinced I could become president of the United States."

"You probably could," Holly said, "but obviously *you're* not too keen on his idea."

Chris turned to Holly, his blue eyes flashing. "That's exactly my point. It was my *father's* idea, not mine. See, he figures we've already got money, so earning more would be pointless. And his brother, my uncle Ron, is a lawyer at the Justice Department. My dad wants me to follow in his footsteps, get my law degree, then run for office. . . . He's got it all planned out."

"And what do *you* want to do?" Holly asked.

Chris sighed. "It'll sound silly, especially compared to being president of the United States."

"It's not silly if it's what *you* want to do," Holly said. "Don't be embarrassed to tell me."

Chris looked up at Holly with a grateful smile. "You won't laugh?"

"Promise."

"I want to be an actor," he said. "Maybe onstage, maybe on TV or in the movies. I'd even do commercials if someone wanted me." He looked up at Holly apologetically, like he still expected her to make fun of him.

"What's wrong with that?" Holly asked.

"Acting's a perfectly respectable profession. And who wouldn't want to be on TV? You could end up being a big star!"

"That's looking on the bright side," Chris said. "My father would call it a pipe dream. He'd say it lacks *substance*. And my family is nothing if not substantial."

"They sound more like prison guards if they won't let you do what you want to," Holly said.

"That's what it feels like," Chris said, opening the mesh bag and pulling out a bunch of grapes. He plucked one and popped it in his mouth. "I've got to get away from them. I wish I could run away to California, like my sister did. She just chucked it all and took off."

Hearing about Chris's parents made Holly appreciate her own more. Sure, her dad was pigheaded about certain things, especially The Mountain and the Franklins, but he'd never told her what to do with her life. Just the opposite. Whatever Holly was interested in, both her parents always gave her their total suppport and encouragement. *You can do anything you put your mind to*, her mother always said.

On the other hand, Holly was just as much a prisoner as Chris was. Only, it wasn't her parents holding her back. It was lupus.

"I'd like to get away, too," Holly confessed, breaking off a piece of the crusty loaf. She rolled over onto her stomach and nibbled on the bread.

"Where would you go?" Chris asked. "What would you do?"

"Well, I haven't narrowed it down yet," Holly said, "but I want to travel all over the world. I'm so curious about other countries, how other people live. I want to study them, learn about them."

"You mean, like, be an anthropologist?" Chris asked.

"Maybe," Holly said. "I'm not just interested in the differences—I want to know what makes people the same, no matter where they live and who they are."

"Cool," Chris said. "I bet you'll do it, too."

"I hope so," Holly said, unable to keep the doubt from creeping into her voice. "Sometimes I'm just not sure." How could she become an anthropologist—or anything else for that matter—when she might not make it to the end of the year? Holly sighed and rolled over onto her back.

"What's the matter?" Chris asked, leaning over her. "You sound so sad."

"Do I?" Holly asked, trying to sound more cheerful.

Chris's face took on that serious, questioning look she'd seen when he'd questioned her about her hat and glasses. His face, too, had such an openness, so much trust and affection she knew was meant only for her. "Is there something you're not telling me?" he asked.

It would have been so easy to tell Chris her secret right now. Just a few little words. *I have lupus.* She had no doubt he'd be sympathetic, concerned, sad at the thought of losing someone he was beginning to feel close to. Holly opened her mouth to speak . . .

. . . and quickly shut it again. She couldn't say it. Not now. It was too nice to feel like a normal girl falling in love, not someone who'd need to be rushed to the hospital at any moment. And even if he was sympathetic, knowing she was so seriously ill was bound to change the way he looked at her. Chris, she was sure, wanted a girlfriend he could have fun with, go places with, look forward to the future with. Not a girl who had no future.

"It's nothing," Holly said, smiling up at him. "I was just thinking how happy I am to be with you, and how I wish this moment never had to end."

"It doesn't have to, Holly," Chris said, his face drawing closer. He plucked a grape and held it to her lips.

Holly let her teeth close over the sweet plumpness, and she closed her eyes. It was so relaxing to be on this soft blanket with Chris so near, to hear the birds singing love songs to each other, to feel the cool mountain breeze bathe her face. She almost believed Chris's words, that this moment could last forever, that forever could last as long as she wanted it to.

Feeling Chris's fingers gently stroking her cheek, Holly opened her eyes and gazed up at him. How could she worry about anything when the moment was so perfect?

Holly felt absolutely weightless as Chris gathered her in his arms and let his lips touch hers. An electric current ran through her body, from her lips to the tips of her fingers and toes. Holly wrapped her arms around Chris and pulled him even closer. She kissed his mouth, his cheek, his neck, his eyes. His lips found hers again and kissed her so softly, so sweetly. Holly felt her mind float away from her body and drift upward, over the mountaintops, toward the cloudless sky.

When Holly became aware again, the sun

was already beginning to set, and the sky was turning pinkish purple. Distant crickets had begun to chirp in a pulsing rhythm. Chris lay her gently against the blanket and gazed down at her peacefully.

"Wow," she said softly. "I've never felt this way before. It was like . . . we were part of the same person. Like there was nothing between us."

"But it's not just physical," Chris agreed. "I feel like I can tell you anything and you'd understand, like I can say things to you I'd never tell anybody else. I feel like I can trust you completely."

Holly's stomach did a sour little twist. How could she possibly tell Chris she felt the same way while she still kept this huge part of herself secret from him? And she couldn't say anything now. It would spoil the mood, the day, the sunset. Maybe the time would come when Holly felt she could trust Chris as much as he trusted her, but the time was definitely not now.

Chapter Fourteen

June's high heels sank into the soft grass as she stumbled around the corner of the dimly lit golf clubhouse. Where was Brett, anyway? It was ten after nine and she'd walked all the way around the cottagelike wooden building twice. She'd killed some time looking in the window of the darkened golf pro shop, she'd taken several walks to the paved driveway that led up to the hotel, and still he hadn't come. Was he standing her up?

June shivered in her black strapless dress. Maybe it had been a stupid idea to wear it since she was meeting Brett outside, but wearing it had been part of her whole scenario. She wanted Brett to see her in it, to see how it flattered her figure. But why hadn't she brought a jacket? June knew how chilly it could get in the evenings. She was beginning to feel a little stupid for coming here at all.

"Psssst! June!"

June peered through the darkness, trying to figure out where the voice was coming from.

Brett emerged from the shadows of the golf course. Tall and lean, he wore a denim jacket, a boxy striped button-down shirt untucked over ripped jeans, and deck shoes with no socks. Now June felt even more foolish for wearing the strapless dress. She felt overdressed and underdressed at the same time.

"Sorry I'm late," he said, leaning down to kiss June on the lips. "We got caught in traffic in Burlington, and then I needed time to change my clothes . . ." Brett paused as he eyed June's bare shoulders. "Whoa!" he said, raising one eyebrow. "You look great! That's a real sexy dress!"

Maybe wearing the dress hadn't been so stupid after all.

"So," Brett said, taking June's hand. "Want to go for a walk?" He took her cold hand in his warm one. "Hey," he said. "You're freezing!" Brett grabbed June around the waist and pulled her closer to his warm body. "How's that?" he asked. "Better?"

June could feel the strong beating of his heart beneath his shirt and the hard muscles of his leg pressing against her thigh. It felt dangerous to be this close to his body with no one else around and nothing but a few layers of clothing between them.

Brett led June up a grassy hill. At the top, June had a view of the golf course. Atop other rises, skinny flagpoles were silhouetted against the starry gray-blue sky. Dark clumps of trees huddled together, and ponds shone silver in the moonlight like scattered coins.

"C'mon," Brett said, leading her down the other side of the hill. He walked fast, and it was hard for June to keep up with him, especially with her heels sinking down at every step.

"Just a minute," June said, leaning over to take off her shoes. Her stockinged feet touched the cold ground, and June's teeth began to chatter. But she didn't say anything to Brett as the two continued across the golf course. If she acted like a spoilsport tonight, he might never ask her out again, and June still had her heart set on the Main Dining Room. Besides, maybe the exercise would warm her up.

Brett led her up another hill to a cluster of trees. "Let's stop here for a minute," he said, taking off his jacket and laying it on the ground. "So you don't get your dress dirty," he added, indicating June should sit on top of it.

June sank gratefully onto the soft denim and pulled the hem of her dress down to cover as much of her chilled legs as possible. Brett sat next to her and put his arm around her shoulder. He began to stroke the bare skin of her back. June felt the goose bumps rise on her flesh, though she wasn't sure if it was excitement at Brett's touch or early frostbite.

"You're still so cold!" Brett exclaimed with concern. "We'll have to do something about that. Here, lie back."

"Lie back?" June asked, confused. "Why?" She couldn't see Brett's face. He was just a fuzzy shape in the darkness, but she had a feeling he was smiling.

"You need to heat up," he said, his voice low and sexy. "And I know just how to do it." There was no mistaking what he meant by that, and June knew she should get up right this minute and ask him to take her home.

June lay back against Brett's jacket and felt damp grass beneath her hair.

Brett lay down beside her and threw one leg over her body, protecting her and pinning her at the same time. Then he lowered his face and pressed his lips against hers. June felt her whole body respond. She arched her back and pressed her lips harder against his. Brett slipped an arm under June's back and slowly began to unzip her dress.

"Hey!" she protested softly. "I thought you were going to keep me warm."

"I am," he said, pulling the zipper all the way down. His warm hand stroked her back while his other hand moved slowly up her thigh, under her dress.

"Brett . . ." June said, but she was silenced by Brett's hot, wet mouth on hers once again. The hand that was on her thigh slipped under the elastic waistband of her stockings and began to pull them down over her hips. Then the hand went away for a moment and June heard Brett unzip his pants.

Though June had had a feeling this might happen, and part of her even wanted it to, this was all going too fast. She barely knew Brett, and he knew even less about her. Part of that was her fault, of course, for not telling him who she really was. Even so, they'd only spent a few hours together. And their date had only started five minutes ago. This was hardly the social debut June had envisioned for herself.

Brett pulled June's stockings down past her knees.

"No, Brett!" June said, grabbing at her stockings and pulling them up again. Then she rolled away from him and sat up, holding her dress to cover her chest.

"What's the matter, June?" Brett asked, sitting up also.

"I'm not ready for this," June said. "I don't even know your last name!"

Brett laughed. "It's Matthews. Anything else you want to know?"

"A lot of things," June said, fumbling behind her back for her zipper. She managed to zip it halfway up. "Like, who are you? What do you want out of life? What are you looking for in a relationship?"

Brett shook his head. "Those are some pretty heavy questions. Can't we talk about that later?"

He began to stroke June's thigh again, and she let him. Why not give Brett what he wanted, especially when she wanted it, too? She'd never been so attracted to a guy, and she knew this could be the most exciting moment of her life. But that was thinking too short-term.

"No, Brett," June said, removing his hand

and standing up. "The thing is, I really like you. And I want to get to know you better. I just don't think this is the best way to start."

Brett sighed and stood up, zipping up his pants. "Too bad," he said. "It would have been great." He leaned down and picked up his jacket.

"I'm sure it would," June said, twisting her dress around halfway so she could zip it the rest of the way up. Then she straightened it out again. "But let's take it slow, okay? Let's talk first. Let's do things together."

"Sure," Brett said. He headed down the hill, out from under the trees.

Grabbing her shoes, June scurried to keep up with him. "You're not mad, are you?" she asked.

Brett slowed down so June could walk by his side. "No," he said. "Just a little disappointed, I guess."

"Don't be," June said. "I still really want to go out with you. We could even do something else right now. Like, why don't we grab a bite to eat?"

Brett contemplated this. "Well, I just got back from dinner, so I'm not really hungry," he said. "And it *is* kind of late. I'm going sailing with some friends early tomorrow morning, so I'd better turn in."

"Oh." June tried not to think about the fact that Brett would have stayed up plenty late with her tonight if she'd been willing to go along with his plan. She tried to blot out of her mind the fact that he was going sailing tomorrow and hadn't invited her. "Well, then let's make a plan for some other time," she said. "How 'bout tomorrow night? Or the next day?"

"Sure," Brett said. "I'll call you."

"But you don't have my number," June pointed out.

Brett stopped walking. "Tell it to me," he said. "I'll remember it and write it down as soon as I get back to my room."

June recited her telephone number for him slowly, then repeated it.

"Got it!" he said. He leaned down and kissed her lightly on the lips. "No hard feelings," he said afterward. "I'll walk you to the front gate."

"Holly!" her mother exclaimed as Holly came through the front door. Peg Paige, sitting on the couch that was too big for the living room, looked panic-stricken. A paperback book lay open on her lap, but Holly had a feeling her mother hadn't been reading it. "Where have you been?" Mrs. Paige demanded. "We've been so worried about you!"

"We thought something had happened," her father put in. He sat in his oversized comfortable chair, feet up on a matching ottoman. The TV was on, but the sound was turned so low Holly could barely hear it.

"We called all the local hospitals," her mother added, "thinking maybe you'd collapsed."

"As you can see for yourselves," Holly said, "I'm perfectly fine." Though she appreciated her parents' concern, this was going too far. Couldn't she just go on a date like a normal girl without her parents' fearing she was dead?

Mrs. Paige got up and walked quickly to Holly's side. "Why didn't you call us?" she asked. "Where were you?"

This was a question Holly had no intention of answering. "I just went for a walk," she said.

"For *seven hours?*" her mother said. "You missed dinner."

Holly thought of the little roadside café Chris had just taken her to. It had looked like a small log cabin, with rough-hewn wooden tables and hand-dipped candles. The owner of the café waited on tables himself in jeans and a flannel shirt. The food had been simple, but there'd been plenty of it—beef stew and potatoes and as much salad as you could eat.

She and Chris had sat there for hours, catching up on the years since sixth grade. Chris had told her about Dover Prep, about his sister's band and how she'd been disowned by his parents, about his family history. Holly had found it very intimidating to learn that Chris's great-grandfather had founded a major railroad and that his grandfather owned Woodruff's, an exclusive chain of department stores. She hadn't wanted to tell Chris about her own, far more modest family history, but he'd dragged it out of her. He'd seemed far more interested in the fact that her great-grandmother had performed in vaudeville than he was in any of his own ancestors.

They'd talked, too, about just picking up and leaving together, traveling cross-country and ending up in Hollywood where Chris could pursue his acting career. It had all been just a fantasy, but it had sure been fun. For hours, Holly had forgotten there was anything wrong with her. But now, here was her mother to remind her.

"I grabbed a bite in town," she said, "So don't worry about me, okay?"

Holly's mother placed her cool hands against Holly's cheeks. "You feel hot," she said. "I think you probably overdid it with the exercise."

"Yeah, Hol," her father said. "You can't go traipsing around town. You're ill. You have to take care of yourself. Why don't you call it a night?"

"Sure," Holly said, giving her mom a peck on the cheek. She couldn't wait to get to her room, anyway. She wanted to block out the fear and the worry again, and just think about Chris—the feel of his arms, the touch of his lips, and that lovely floating sensation that made her feel as if gravity didn't have any power over her at all.

She was falling in love with him, no doubt about it. And for the first time since she'd met him, Holly saw no reason to stop herself.

Chris didn't even bother to turn on the lights of his room. He just fell into bed, against the six fluffy pillows his mother insisted on keeping just for decoration, and gazed out the window at the starry sky. The window was open, and a chilly breeze blew in, carrying with it the smell of pine needles, cedar, and violets. It was the smell of this afternoon, the smell of Holly, the smell of being in love.

The past seven hours had been the happiest of Chris's life. He'd just dropped off Holly at her door, yet he already couldn't wait to see her again. He thought of calling her, but remembered her parents were home. What if one of them picked up the phone? Chris thought of giving a false name, pretending to be someone else, but that would spoil the wonderful feeling that still carried him along.

There was just one niggling thought at the back of Chris's mind, something that had been bothering him ever since Holly had shown up at the tennis courts the other day. It was the big hat and sunglasses she wore, and the way she tried to avoid his questions whenever he asked her about them. Holly wasn't a spy, of course, but she *was* hiding something. What was it? And was it something that was going to get in the way of their growing feelings for each other?

What *was* it? Chris's heart lurched as he thought of a possible answer. What if there was another guy in the picture? What if Holly already had a boyfriend? A girl as beautiful as she was had to be involved with someone. And that would explain why she was always covering herself up. She didn't want anyone to recognize her with Chris. It would also explain why Holly had kept putting him off when he asked her out.

Chris leaped out of bed and strode to the window. So who was this guy? Someone from town? Someone he might still remember from grade school? Chris tried to picture the kind of guy Holly might go for. Maybe someone bigger than he was, a guy with major muscle groups, a tough guy, a guy who rode a motorcycle. Or maybe some real intellectual interested in the same things she was—travel and culture and anthropology. No matter who he was, though, Chris was sure the guy couldn't feel as strongly about Holly as he did. Chris wanted to see this guy face-to-face and tell him to back off.

There was a knock at the door.

"Who is it?" Chris asked.

The lights came on, and Chris blinked at the brightness.

"Why are you standing here in the dark?" his mother asked, entering the room. She wore silk pin-striped pajamas and monogrammed bedroom slippers.

Chris shrugged. "Just thinking, I guess."

His mother approached. "Thinking about who you're inviting to your birthday party, I hope."

"You might say that."

Mrs. Franklin sat on the window seat. "The party's only a few days away," she reminded him, "and I don't want to be rude to Chuck Durham's daughter. If we're going to invite her, we can't wait any longer."

The time had come to stand up to his mother, and this time Chris was ready. "I'm not inviting Hilary," he said.

His mother's face went blank. "You're not? Then who—"

"Holly Paige," he said. "I've already asked her, and she said yes."

Mrs. Franklin's furrowed forehead wrinkled even more. "Paige . . . Paige . . . Do we know them?"

There was no point holding back information. His parents were bound to figure it out sooner or later. "She's from town," Chris said. "Her dad was mayor here ten years—"

Mrs. Franklin gasped. "*Tom* Paige? The one who fought against The Mountain?"

"That's the one," Chris said.

Mrs. Franklin shook her head firmly. "No,"

she said. "Your father will never go for that. And neither do I. I mean, who *is* this girl? Doesn't she wait tables at her mother's diner?"

"So what if she does?" Chris asked defensively. "What's wrong with working hard? That's what Dad's always telling us to do, right?"

"This is completely different," his mother said, standing up. "And you know what I mean. What sort of prospects does a girl like that have? What right does she have to expect someone of your caliber to be interested in her?"

"She has every right!" Chris shouted.

Chris's mother looked at him sympathetically. "You're still young, Chris," she said, "and I understand how strong feelings at this age can cancel out your better judgment. So trust me on this one. Tell this girl you're very sorry, but you made a mistake."

Chris had never wanted to strike anyone in his entire life, certainly not his mother. But he felt his hands clench into fists. It took every ounce of self-control he had to keep them pressed against his sides. "I won't do it," he said, his voice shaking. "It's *not* a mistake. She's the girl I want to be with."

Now his mother got angry. "Don't you even care how *I* feel?" she demanded. "Do you realize how much time and money I've spent on this party, inviting just the right people to launch your career? And now you want to throw it all away by snubbing Chuck Durham's daughter and showing up with some little nothing?"

Chris slammed his fist against the wall, causing it to shake. "She's not a 'little nothing' and don't you ever say that again!" he yelled.

"Don't you raise your voice to me," his mother warned.

Chris didn't even hear her. "And I thought this was *my* birthday! My party!" he shouted. "But obviously what *I* want has never mattered to you or Dad."

"You know that's not true," his mother objected.

"Oh, yeah?" Chris challenged her. "Then I'm holding you to it. Either you let me invite Holly, or I'm not going."

"But you *have* to come . . ." his mother said.

"I don't have to do anything anymore," Chris said. "These are my terms, and this is *my* life. Take it or leave it."

Chris folded his arms across his chest and stared his mother down. Never in his life had he stood up to either of his parents this way, and it felt great. The blood pounded through his veins and he was breathing hard and fast, as if he'd just finished running a marathon.

Chris's mother stared back at him, her jaw slack, her eyes wide with surprise. "I never said you couldn't choose your own date," she said. "If you insist on bringing this girl, that's your right."

Chris smiled in triumph.

"But of course I'll have to mention this to your father," Mrs. Franklin said, "and I don't think *he's* going to be very happy."

Chris's mood deflated at the thought of facing his father. His mother's anger was nothing compared to his father's six feet four inches of pride and fury. But Chris wasn't going to back down now. He'd made his decision. And his family was going to go along with it whether they liked it or not.

"I'm in love!" June announced dramatically, closing the bedroom door behind her.

Holly, who lay in bed reading, looked up from her book. June's strapless black dress was wrinkled and her shoulders were streaked with dirt. And were those bits of grass in June's tousled hair?

"How was your date with Brett?" Holly asked with a worried frown. "Did you get to eat in the Main Dining Room?"

"Not yet," June said, kicking off her shoes. She spun her dress around her body and unzipped it. "But next time for sure."

Holly put her book down and sat up. "Where'd he take you?"

June slipped out of her dress and threw it on her bed. "Well, we just went for a walk, but it was really romantic. I *know* he's interested in me. He couldn't keep his hands off me!"

"That's nice, I guess," Holly said.

June grabbed her pink terry-cloth bathrobe off a hook on the wall and put it on. "Not that I want to say 'I told you so,'" she said, "but Brett knows who I really am now, and it didn't change a thing. He still wanted to go out with me!"

"Really?" Holly asked, surprised. "How did he find out?"

June quickly related her run-in with Mrs. Donnely and described how Brett had saved her.

Holly shook her head in disbelief. Maybe she wasn't as good a judge of character as she'd thought. Maybe she'd judged Brett too harshly. He *had* brought her a soda at the movie theater, and Chris liked him. That had to count for something. "I'm sorry I doubted you," she told her sister. "Maybe fairy tales *do* come true. I think mine is, too."

June came over to Holly's bed and sat down. "Tell me all about it!" she said excitedly. "Did you hear from Chris?"

Holly described the romantic afternoon and evening they'd spent together and told June about Chris's invitation to his birthday party. June threw her arms around Holly and hugged her.

"This is so exciting!" she squealed. "Things are turning out so well for both of us! I wonder if I can get Brett to invite me as *his* date to the party?"

June's enthusiasm was catching. "We could double-date!" Holly said enthusiastically. "Maybe after the party we could all drive into Burlington and hit some of the clubs."

"Wouldn't that be great?" June asked, bouncing up and down on Holly's mattress.

Holly couldn't remember the last time she'd felt so hopeful, so excited. Her spirit felt light and free. She felt like a kid again. She felt as if she had a whole life of happiness to look forward to. Even the fantasy she shared with Chris of running away and seeing the world together seemed like it might come true. Tonight, it seemed like anything was possible.

Chapter Fifteen

"Next, please," called the bank clerk with the pudgy face and bald head.

Chris, who was next on line at Landon Savings & Loan, walked up to the worn wooden counter. The bank looked exactly the same as it had twelve years ago when Chris had first opened his bank account with pennies and nickels he'd saved from his piggy bank. Other folks who'd lived here a lot longer had told him it looked the same as it had the day it opened a hundred years ago.

An intricately carved wooden counter extended along the back wall with four teller's stations behind wrought-iron gates. In the center of the small open area was a matching wooden table with a marble top for filling out deposit and withdrawal slips. A creaky wooden door led to the back. And that was all. There were no automatic teller machines, no video screens, nothing more high-tech than the calculators the clerks used to add up deposits and withdrawals.

"Hi," Chris said to the clerk, whose nameplate read JOE. Chris slipped his paycheck and deposit slip under the iron gate. It was only a few hundred dollars, a week's salary for teaching tennis at the hotel, but this money meant more to Chris than any trust fund his father had set up for him. This paycheck, and every penny in his account here, was money Chris had earned himself. Already he'd saved up five thousand dollars.

It felt good to know he had money that was totally his, money that proved he could make it on his own if he had to, without his parents' help. If Blaire could do it, why couldn't he? Sure, Blaire was struggling financially, but she wasn't starving. The most important thing was that Blaire was her own person. No one told her what to do anymore. That was worth a whole lot more than money.

While the clerk processed his deposit slip, Chris's eyes wandered. Someone named Joshua had carved his name in the wooden counter in 1947. A cobweb hung between two

bars of the teller's gate. There was a small, cy-
lindrical container with a little slot on top, sitting on the ledge. Chris picked up the
container and read the writing on it.

It said HELP SAVE HOLLY PAIGE! in big red
letters.

Chris stared at the container for a second,
not understanding. Holly Paige? *His* Holly?
What did this mean? Chris shook the container, and it jingled. There seemed to be a few
coins inside.

"Excuse me," Chris said, showing the container to the clerk. "Do you know what this is
for?"

The clerk looked up. "Oh, that!" he said. "I
don't know why that's still out. The collection
ended a few months ago."

"What collection?" Chris asked.

"For Holly," the clerk said. "Her medical
bills went sky high. The whole town chipped in
to help her parents pay for it. Not that it was
enough, of course, but it helped."

Chris gripped the iron rails and stared at
the clerk. "Wait a minute, wait a minute," he
said. "First of all, is this the Holly Paige whose
mother owns Peg's Diner?"

The clerk nodded.

"And she was sick?"

"I thought everybody knew," the clerk said with surprise. "She's got lupus. I don't really understand the disease, myself, but I hear it's pretty serious."

Lupus. Chris had known of a girl who had it, the sister of one of his friends from Dover. But it hadn't been life-threatening. Her face had just gotten puffy for a while. Then the doctors gave her steroids and she went back to normal.

So why had the whole town made a big thing about Holly? Holly looked completely normal. And the clerk had said the collection was over. Maybe that meant Holly didn't have the disease anymore. Like his friend's sister. That had to be it.

"I guess she's all better now, huh?" Chris asked.

The clerk shrugged. "They say she's in remission. But she was in the hospital all last year. Couldn't even get out of bed, I heard. And what she's got could come back anytime and get much worse."

"How much worse?" Chris asked, afraid to hear the answer.

The sad expression in the clerk's eyes answered Chris's question. "It's a real shame, too," the clerk said. "Such a nice girl. Always takes my lunch order at the diner." The clerk shook his head. "Such a shame."

Chris's legs felt so weak, he had to clutch the iron bars to keep from falling. How could Holly be sick, sick enough to die? They'd just taken a hike together yesterday and had a romantic dinner. She was coming to his birthday party. They'd talked about running away together. Holly was *alive*. He was in love with her. She couldn't die!

Then Chris thought about how tired Holly had been while they were hiking. She'd been breathing hard and hadn't been able to keep up. And she'd seemed so defensive about it. Chris thought about the hat and sunglasses, too. Maybe it was all tied in together. Maybe it wasn't a boyfriend she was hiding. Maybe it was the fact that she didn't have long to live.

"You okay?" the clerk asked, slipping a copy of Chris's deposit slip back under the gate.

Chris took the slip and jammed it in the pocket of his tennis shorts. "Yeah, sure," he said, wandering away. He didn't know what to do, where to go, what to say to Holly the next time he saw her. He needed time to think.

*   *   *

June had showered for half an hour in the ladies' locker room and shampooed her hair three times, but it was impossible to wash away the smell of disinfectant. Or maybe the smell was just stuck in her nostrils after four straight days of breathing it in. Her back was beginning to ache, too, from bending over toilets and bathtubs as she scrubbed them. Did the guests even appreciate all her hard work? Or did they just take it for granted that their rooms would be spotless without ever wondering how they'd gotten that way?

Sitting on an upholstered bench by the row of polished teak lockers, June finished towel-drying her hair and threw the towel into a canvas bin. She still wasn't supposed to be using guest facilities, of course, but she'd stopped caring. She'd even stopped bringing her wig. Now that Brett knew who she was, what difference did it make? And she deserved *some* small luxury in exchange for her hard work.

June grabbed her clothes out of her locker. She'd borrowed a khaki skirt and white cotton blouse from Holly and bought a white stretchy headband from the golf pro shop at lunchtime. After putting these on with her white canvas sneakers, June studied her reflection in the wall of full-length mirrors. Then she smiled. With this outfit, and without the red wig, she looked even more like a guest of the hotel. She looked even more like the kind of girl Brett would go out with. Now all she had to do was find him so he could ask her on another date, hopefully to Chris's birthday party.

She had looked for him all during lunch before she'd remembered he'd said he was going sailing today. But maybe he was back now. It was already dinnertime. June would just take a stroll around the hotel and see if she just happened to bump into him.

After checking out the Terrace Café, she looked in Samurai, the hotel's Japanese restaurant. She wandered through Ricardo's, the Italian eatery, and ended up at the entrance to the Main Dining Room. If he wasn't here, there was no place else to look.

Taking a deep breath, June marched past the tuxedoed maître d' and entered the palatial hall. A giant crystal chandelier hung in the center of the room over a bubbling marble fountain with a statue of Venus in the center. Surrounding the fountain were round tables covered with snowy white linen tablecloths and set with white china dishes rimmed with gold.

Silver cutlery and crystal goblets completed the place settings, and every table had a huge arrangement of white roses in the center.

It was early, only six-thirty, so many of the tables were empty. Still, it was worth taking a look around just in case Brett was here.

"Excuse me," said a busboy in a snotty voice. He wore a white dinner jacket and black bow tie and didn't look much older than June. "May I help you?"

June blushed as she realized what the *real* guests were wearing. The men wore jackets and ties, and the women looked elegant in silk dresses and pearls. No wonder this guy had stopped her. "I'm, uh, meeting someone," she said, hurrying away.

She passed a large table with two gray-haired grandparents, a middle-aged couple, and three little boys who wore jackets and ties and ate with perfect table manners. There was a table of men in their thirties, talking and laughing and drinking champagne. Then June spotted Brett wearing a navy blue blazer and a red-and-blue striped tie. June almost didn't recognize him all dressed up. She'd only seen him in his bathing suit or in his untucked shirt and jeans last night. He looked adorable this way, too.

But who was the person he was with? June could only see the back of someone's head, a female head, with dirty-blond, straight, shoulder-length hair. Could that be Brett's mother? June took a few steps closer until she could hear what they were saying.

". . . you brought the boat about so fast, I thought I was going to fall in!" the blonde was saying. Her voice was young and light, like a teenager's. June had a very strong feeling this wasn't Brett's mother.

Brett grinned mischievously. "That was the whole idea!" he said. "I wanted to see what you'd look like in a wet T-shirt."

"Brett!" the girl protested.

This was *definitely* not Brett's mother. June positioned herself behind a tall potted ficus tree so she could get a look at the girl's face and hear more.

The girl wasn't exactly pretty, but she looked fresh and natural with ruddy pink splotches on her cheeks. She had a small, straight nose, pale green eyes, and blond lashes. "You are so bad," the girl said, chucking Brett under the chin. "I don't know why I go out with you."

June's face grew hot. *Go out with?* Brett had never mentioned he was dating her or anybody else. And this must have been the "friend" he went sailing with today.

"Fine," Brett said, shrugging playfully. "Don't go out with me, then. I'll find someone else to take to Chris's birthday party."

"Very funny," the girl said. "You know I already blew five hundred on a dress that *you* helped me pick out."

June wanted to bury herself in the dirt that surrounded the ficus tree. So much for Brett inviting *her* to Chris's birthday party. This girl was more than just a date. She must be Brett's *girlfriend*. So what had June's date with Brett last night been all about? June felt her face grow even hotter as the answer grew clear.

As far as Brett was concerned, June wasn't good enough to go on a *real* date with, to show off to people he knew in the Main Dining Room. No, June was just a townie girl. A lowly maid. A plaything he could fool around with in the shadows, then drop when he was done with her. June hated to admit it, but Holly had been absolutely right about him.

And it didn't say much about Brett that he was willing to have sex with June when he already had a girlfriend. June was furious with herself that she'd almost let him. She'd been a fool, a stupid, innocent fool who'd let her fantasies run away with her.

"Excuse me." It was the snotty busboy again, looking down his freckled nose at her. "Did you find—"

"Yes!" June cut him off before he could make her feel any lower, any less welcome here, than she already felt. "I was just leaving," she said, with as much dignity as she could muster.

Chapter Sixteen

June knelt by Holly's feet, her mouth so full of pins she resembled a porcupine. Holly looked down to see how June was doing with the hem of her new turquoise crushed-velvet dress. Actually, it wasn't a *new* dress. She'd picked it up this afternoon at her favorite thrift shop in Burlington. The dress was sleeveless with a square neckline. Fitted through the bodice, it flared outward at the hips and reached all the way to the floor, even with the high heels she was wearing. June was rapidly pinning up the hem to mid-calf length.

"Very fifties," June declared after removing the pins from her mouth. "Very Grace Kelly."

Grace Kelly, an American movie star, had married the Prince of Monaco. Maybe Holly had found her prince, too. She spun around so the dress puffed outward like a bell. "I feel like Cinderella!" she declared.

"And I feel like the attic mice who helped Cinderella make her dress," June said ruefully.

Holly was instantly sorry she'd said anything about how happy she was. It could only make June feel worse about what had happened with Brett. While Holly hadn't been surprised to hear she'd been right about him all along, she would have much rather been wrong. That way June might have something wonderful to look forward to, too.

"I wish you were going to the party," she said. "It won't be as much fun if you're not there."

June looked up in surprise. "Didn't I tell you? I guess we've been so busy with the dress, I forgot. I'm working the party tonight."

"Working?"

"As a waitress. Mrs. Donnely told me this morning that the dining room was short-staffed. I'll be serving you hors d'oeuvres."

"Oh, June," Holly said, sinking to her knees beside her sister. "Are you sure you want to do that? You wanted to be a *guest*."

June shrugged. "I really don't mind. It pays

well, and it's almost as good as being invited. After I'm done serving, maybe I'll slip on my wig and mingle."

Holly's shocked look was met with laughter.

"Just kidding!" June said, pushing lightly against Holly's shoulder. "Can't you take a joke? Don't worry, Hol. I'm getting used to the idea that waiting on these people is the closest *I'll* ever get to high society. Now take this off so I can hem it."

Holly pulled down the side zipper and stepped out of the dress. Then she tried to kick off her shoes, but they were fitting so tight tonight they wouldn't come off. "That's funny," Holly said, sitting on her bed. She tugged at one black suede high heel until she was able to pry it off. Her foot was puffy and swollen, and her ankle looked thicker than normal. Her other foot was just as bad. "Guess I've been spending too much time on my feet lately," she told her sister.

June looked up from the floor where she sat threading a needle with turquoise thread. "That's what we've all been trying to tell you," she said. "You don't have to prove you're Super Woman, Hol. Even people who *aren't* sick rest once in a while."

"I'm not *sick*," Holly insisted. "I'm in *remis-*

sion. And I feel fine. Even people who aren't sick get tired once in a while."

June didn't look convinced.

"Tell you what," Holly said, swinging her feet up onto the bed. "I'll lie here like a princess while you hem my dress. Will that make you happy?"

"Actually, it will," June said, knotting the thread.

"You're no fun." Holly stifled a yawn.

June sighed, and Holly felt bad again for being so insensitive. How could she expect June to be "fun" after she'd just gotten her heart broken?

"You still thinking about Brett?" Holly asked.

June shrugged as she began to sew Holly's hem. "Mostly I'm just thinking about how stupid I've been. You saw what was going on. Why couldn't I?"

"It's harder when you really like somebody," Holly said. "Sometimes you see only what you want to see."

"But it was all there in front of my eyes," June said. "When I think about some of the things he said . . . like, 'I don't care what your name is—you're a hot girl and we have fun together.' I could have been anybody, as far as he was concerned. I was just a body and a pair of lips."

"A lot of guys are like that," Holly pointed out. "And not just rich ones."

"I know," June said, "but I think Brett's money was shining in my eyes so bright, I couldn't see anything else. I've learned my lesson, though. That's the last time I fall for *anybody* so quick, rich or not."

Holly smiled. She'd heard this from June about a thousand times before. That's why she wasn't *too* worried whether or not June would recover from her disappointment. June always bounced back, and it never took too long.

"Is Chris picking you up?" June asked, turning the skirt as she continued hemming.

"No, I'm driving myself," Holly said. "I don't want Mom and Dad to see his car outside."

"So you still haven't told them you're seeing him?" June asked, looking up.

Holly shook her head. "I can't."

"Then how are you going to explain where you're going tonight?"

"I've already told them I'm going to a friend's birthday party. They didn't ask any questions."

"And how does Chris feel about your keeping from him this big secret?"

"That's the funny thing," Holly said. "We haven't really talked about it. We haven't talked about much of anything since I saw him Wednesday night."

"Hasn't he called you?"

"He stopped by the diner for a minute this afternoon, just to confirm for tonight. But then he had to go. He was acting a little weird. I hope he's not sorry he invited me."

"I'm sure that's not it," June said. "Do you know how many people are coming to this party? Over three hundred! He probably just had to help his mother with the details."

Holly nodded and leaned back against her pillow. "Three hundred rich people who'll be looking down their noses at me." She yawned and rolled over onto her side. "If I weren't so tired, I'd be a lot more nervous about facing them. Not to mention Chris's parents."

"You'll do fine," June said. "And remember, if anybody tries to make you feel bad, you just call on me. I'll bombard 'em with stuffed mushrooms and skewer 'em with toothpicks!"

Holly chuckled and closed her eyes. "You're a great sister, June," she murmured as she dropped off to sleep.

*   *   *

The Main Dining Room was a sea of black and white. Men in tuxedos and starched white shirts chatted with women wearing black cocktail dresses and strands of gleaming pearls. Tables covered with white linen cloths rimmed one side of the polished oval floor. A white stone fountain occupied the center of the room. Its burbling water accompanied the strains of a big-band orchestra on a stage at the far end of the room. Waiters and waitresses in white shirts and black pants pushed politely through the crowd, offering silver trays of hors d'oeuvres.

Holly self-consciously smoothed the turquoise crushed-velvet bodice of her thrift-shop dress. She was the only spot of color in the room. A few hours ago, Holly had felt like Cinderella. Now she felt like a tacky fake jewel in the middle of Tiffany's.

One of the tuxedos detached itself from a group near the door and headed toward her. It took a second for Holly to recognize him as Chris. He looked taller, somehow, though maybe it was just that Holly had never seen him so dressed up. His hair gleamed golden in the light of the crystal chandelier, and his face was lightly sunburned. He looked gorgeous and, unlike her, completely at home with these people.

"Holly," he greeted her, a strained smile on his face.

Chris must have noticed it, too, how silly she looked, how out of place. He was probably thinking his parents had been right about her all along. He was probably sorry he'd invited her. Holly was beginning to feel sorry, too, that she'd come.

"Hi," she said shyly, looking down.

There was an awkward pause. Holly racked her brains trying to think of the best way to get out of this gracefully. She really was feeling tired, despite a two-hour nap. And her ankles and feet still looked so puffy, she was beginning to regret June had shortened her dress. Maybe she should tell Chris she wasn't feeling well and go home.

"We need to talk," Chris said in a serious voice.

Holly nodded. Her worst fears were coming true. Chris was going to ask her to leave before she even had the chance to excuse herself.

"Let's go for a walk on the terrace," Chris said, taking her arm.

His touch was gentle. Holly was surprised he was going to so much trouble to let her down. Chris led her across the crowded floor where couples munched tiny slices of toast with bits of salmon and delicate chunks of chicken wrapped with bacon.

A very tall man with thinning blond hair stepped in front of them, blocking their path. Next to him was a plumpish woman with a leathery tan face and blond bouffant hairdo. "Well, Chris?" the man asked. His voice was cold. "Aren't you going to introduce us?"

Chris glared up at the man. "Of course," he said politely, though his tone was no warmer. "Dad, Mom, I'd like you to meet my date, Holly Paige."

Holly felt a steel clamp tighten around her heart. She'd thought no one could seem less happy to see her than Chris, but she'd been wrong. Mr. Franklin extended an enormous hand and shook hers briefly. "How do you do," was all he said.

Mrs. Franklin extended her hand, too. When Holly took it, it was limp and lifeless. "Hello, Holly," she said. Then she glanced at the door and became suddenly animated. "Oh, look, Bill!" she exclaimed. "There's Chuck Durham and his lovely daughter, Hilary. Let's go over and say hello."

With only a brief nod to Holly, the two were on their way.

"Don't mind them," Chris muttered as he took her arm again and led her to the French doors that lined one long wall of the room. "They're jerks."

Holly was surprised Chris was being so sympathetic. But then again, he was still a nice person, even if he'd realized he and Holly were wrong for each other. Chris pushed open one of the French doors and held it open for Holly to pass through.

The white stone terrace was semicircular with a low stone railing. It overlooked the floodlit turquoise swimming pool around which more party guests strolled. In the distance, silhouetted against the darker mountains, were the rolling hills of the golf course. Holly and Chris paused by the railing and looked out over the view. It was all so peaceful, so beautiful. An unlikely setting for the bad news Chris was about to break.

"Why didn't you tell me?" Chris asked in a low, anguished voice.

Holly looked at him, startled. "Tell you what?"

Chris's face was a mask of pain. "You don't have to hide it anymore, Holly," he said. "I already know."

This wasn't going the way Holly had expected. "What are you talking about?" she asked.

"I saw the collection can," Chris said, his voice breaking. "At the bank."

Holly froze. The collection cans! She'd thought they'd disappeared months ago. But what did she expect in such a small town? She should have realized her secret would come out no matter what she did to prevent it.

"Why didn't you tell me?" Chris repeated, gazing at Holly with burning eyes. "I poured my heart out to you. I told you my most secret thoughts, things I've never told another living soul. I trusted you."

"You can still trust me," Holly assured him. "I wouldn't repeat anything you said."

"That's not what I mean!" Chris said, grabbing her shoulders. "I thought we were sharing something. I thought you were being as open with me as I was with you. But you were holding out on me, Holly. How could you not tell me about such an important piece of your life?"

Holly almost wanted to laugh at the absurdity of it all. Chris had no right to be angry. *She* was the one who'd been cheated of a healthy life, not him. And what was so terrible about wanting to forget, just for a little while, that she was doomed?

"You don't understand," Holly said, taking a few steps away from Chris. It was hard to walk with her shoes so tight and her ankles so swollen. She leaned against the railing for support.

Chris stuck to her side. "Explain it to me," he said. "I *want* to understand."

Holly turned and glanced up at him. Chris was giving her the same pitying look she'd seen on the faces of everyone she knew these past twelve months. The look that said "Poor Holly's going to die and it's so sad but thank God it's not me." It was so easy to feel sorry for someone from the safety of your own health. Didn't any of them realize sympathy like that didn't do her any good?

"Yes, I'm sick," Holly said, tears brimming in her eyes. "I'm sick of feeling hopeless. I'm sick of people treating me like an invalid. I'm sick of trying to pretend that everything's going to be okay. I'm sick of being Landon's favorite charity case!"

Chris nodded. "I can understand that."

"Can you?" Holly demanded. "Then why can't you understand that for once, just once, I wanted someone *not* to know I had lupus? Why can't you understand that I wanted to be treated like a regular person for a change?" Holly was practically screaming, and several other guests on the patio turned to look at her curiously. Holly knew she should keep her voice down, not make a scene, not give Chris's parents even more reason to look down on her. But she was past caring. A sob tore through her throat, wracking her entire body.

Chris's arms were instantly around her. Warm, comforting, shielding her against everything and everybody. His soft hands were stroking her hair. His cheeks were wet with tears. "I *do* understand," he said softly, insistently. "I just wanted you to explain it to me. I wanted to know I was important enough in your life that you'd tell me what was really going on."

The sobs had taken over now. Holly couldn't even answer. All she could do was bury herself inside of Chris's protective embrace.

"I've never cared about anyone as much as I care about you," Chris whispered into her hair. "And if we're going to spend the rest of our lives together, we have to be completely honest with each other."

Chris's words shocked Holly out of her tears. Had she heard right? Had he really said what she'd thought he just said? Holly looked up at Chris with shining eyes. Chris, too, looked stunned, like he couldn't believe what had just slipped out of his mouth. Then his expression became resolute.

"I mean it, Holly," he said firmly. "I've never been able to put it into words before, even to myself. But ever since I ran into you again, I've been looking at everything differently. I feel like I'm seeing my life clearly for the first time."

"What do you see?" Holly asked.

"I see how my parents have kept me in a choke hold," Chris began. "I see that it *is* possible for me to strike out on my own. And that's what I plan to do. With you."

"What do you mean—strike out?"

"We have the power to make our fantasies come true," Chris said, staring over Holly's head at the distant, glowing half-moon. "We've been dreaming about hitting the road and seeing the world together. Why don't we stop talking about it and *really* do it?"

"You mean pack our bags? Just hop in your car, take off, and leave everybody?"

"You got it."

Holly laughed. "You're crazy! We can't do that."

"Why not?" Chris had a wild look in his eyes and his face was flushed. It seemed to be catching, too. Holly's own heart was beginning to beat faster as adrenaline filled her veins. She had to talk him out of this before they got carried away.

"What about Yale?" she asked. "You can't give that up. And I've got my job, my family, not to mention doctor appointments."

"There are doctors all over the world," Chris said. "We'll find good ones for you to see. Specialists. The best."

Holly shook her head. This wasn't working. She tried another tack. "We're practically strangers," she pointed out. "Even if we did torture each other in sixth grade, we've really only known each other a week."

"We've got the rest of our lives to get to know each other."

There was that phrase again. "That's the biggest point of all," Holly argued. "The rest of our lives might not be too long, at least not in my case. What kind of future could we have together?"

"That's exactly why we *should* go," Chris insisted. "Even if we don't have forever, we have *right now*. If this is our only chance, we can't waste it." Chris held Holly to his chest so tightly, she was almost afraid he'd crush her. "At least think about it, Holly," he begged. "We owe it to each other."

Chris made it all sound so clear, so simple. This idea that had sounded so crazy a moment ago was beginning to sound real, possible.

"C'mon," Chris said, breaking away from her and taking her hand. "They're playing a slow song. You can think about it while we dance."

Chapter Seventeen

"Would you care for a shrimp ball?" June loudly asked the elderly man with the hearing aid. The few remaining strands of white hair on the left side of his head had been combed upward to cover his bald skull but only made it halfway.

The old man gave June a denture-smile and poked his toothpick into the batter-dipped hors d'oeuvre. "Thank you!" he said, popping it in his mouth.

June moved on to a group of young debutantes in nearly identical black cocktail dresses. Some of their dresses were a little above the knee, some a little below. Some had short sleeves, some had none, and one had a black rosette at the hip. Was that what it took to fit in with these people? To look so much like everyone else that no one could tell you apart?

"Shrimp ball?" June asked. The debutantes unanimously shook their heads.

"No, thanks," one of them said. "We're on a diet."

June shrugged and moved behind a potted ficus. So much the better. Now there were more for her! She popped a shrimp ball in her mouth and chewed it quickly. It tasted so good! So did the mini quiches and salmon toast and goose-liver pâté she'd snuck off some of her other trays. Of course, she was breaking another rule by eating food meant for guests, but they'd never miss it. There had to be five hundred trays of hors d'oeuvres in the kitchen.

"Are you sure I can't get you some punch?" a male voice asked from the other side of the ficus tree. "I hear it's terrific."

June knew that voice all too well. Peering through the leaves, she saw Brett with the blond girl he'd gone sailing with two days ago. Brett looked striking in his tuxedo, his glossy black hair exactly matching his shiny black satin cummerbund. The girl looked like one of the debutantes who'd just refused a shrimp ball, though her dress was a few inches shorter.

"You spoil me," the girl said, stroking Brett's arm. "You've been fetching and carrying for me all night."

"You're worth it," Brett said, taking hold of the girl's hand and kissing the back of it. "I shall return."

He took off in the direction of a long table with two large crystal punch bowls. Waitresses stood behind the bowls, ladling the bright red punch into crystal goblets.

June sighed. Brett had been gallant with *her* once, before he'd known who she really was. But now that June knew who Brett really was, she almost didn't care. Brett's girlfriend wandered over to the dieting debutantes, who greeted her with squeals and hugs. Brett, meanwhile, was leaning against the punch table, whispering something to the waitress.

June knew that waitress. Her name was Elaine and she was another maid filling in for the evening. Elaine and June had gone to high school together, and Elaine's father owned the filling station on the outskirts of town.

Elaine was laughing now and whispering something to Brett, who was smiling. June felt a cold chill wash through her veins. She had a very strong feeling she knew what was going on, but she had to get closer to be sure. Holding her tray up in front of her face, June made her way through the crowd until she could hear Brett and Elaine's conversation.

"We could go for a walk later," Brett said, looking deeply into Elaine's eyes. "A moonlit romantic stroll. How does that sound?"

Elaine smiled coyly. "Sounds nice. Where shall we meet?"

"The golf clubhouse?" Brett suggested. "Say, around midnight?"

Elaine nodded. "I'll be there."

June smiled a cold, grim smile. Now she'd seen all of Brett's tricks and she understood him perfectly. Girls like Elaine and her, local girls, were like paper towels to him. Just something to wipe his hands on and throw away. But Elaine didn't know this yet. Elaine was gazing at Brett the way June had just a few days ago.

Elaine was a nice girl. June couldn't let her fall into Brett's groping hands. June had to stop Brett before this went any further. And she knew exactly how she was going to do it.

"I only have eyes . . ." Chris crooned along with the big-band singer, ". . . for you, dear . . ."

Holly, whose arms were clasped tightly

around Chris's waist, gazed up at Chris and laughed. He had a nice voice, a deep mellow baritone, but he was making silly faces and wiggling his eyebrows. "You're lucky I'm not a talent scout," she joked.

"Why?" Chris asked, spinning her around before settling back into a relaxed sway, their bodies so comfortably merged together.

"Are you saying you wouldn't give me a part in your movie, despite my unbelievable good looks?"

Holly smiled. "Well, if I were looking for a comedian type, you know, a goofy sidekick, I might give you a shot."

Chris pretended to be hurt. "Is that all you think of me? Just some goofball not to be taken seriously?"

"A *cute* goofball," Holly offered.

Chris's joking expression vanished. "Seriously?"

"Seriously what?"

Chris stopped swaying, though he still held Holly as tightly as ever. "What do you really think of me?" he asked. "I've said so much about how I feel about you. I've made it clear I want to be with you every minute. But you haven't said much at all. Am I wasting my time here, Holly? Is this just another one of my pipe dreams?"

Holly heaved a deep, complicated sigh. She'd tried for so long to be strong, to resist the idea of falling in love, to be realistic about her chances with a guy like Chris. But like an armored tank with all his guns blazing, Chris had run over all her defenses, destroying them completely. There was no use in fighting anymore. The only thing left was to tell him the simple truth.

"I'm falling in love with you," she confessed. It had come out so easily, like simply exhaling a breath of air. "There. I said it," she said, staring into the pearl buttons of his pleated white shirt.

Chris tilted her chin upward so she was staring right into his eyes. His face was now completely animated, glowing with happiness. "I love you, too, Holly," he said. "And I always will. I don't care what you say about how long we've known each other. It's the truest, realest feeling I've ever had in my life. I feel it in every cell of my body."

Holly sighed and leaned against his strong chest. She felt deeply at peace, like her whole life was falling into place. But even now she couldn't completely relax into her happiness. There was always that demon lurking in a dark corner, a demon wielding a sharp knife that could tear her happiness to shreds at any moment. It was bad enough Holly had to live with it every moment. How could she ask Chris to deal with it, too?

"You don't know what you're getting yourself into," Holly warned as they swayed to the music. "What's the point of loving me when you could lose me at any time? Don't love me, Chris," she begged. "It will only be harder on you when I die. And on me, too. How can I leave this earth knowing I'm leaving you behind?"

"Don't think that way!" Chris said fiercely, backing away from Holly so he could look down into her face. "You're not going anywhere without me. And I'm not going anywhere without you. Say you'll travel with me, Holly. We could leave tomorrow, or next week. Just tell me when. I'm not taking no for an answer."

It would be so easy to give Chris the answer he wanted. It was what Holly wanted, too, more than anything. But before she could say yes, she had to make sure Chris truly understood what he was in for. "It might seem easy to love me now," Holly warned, "while I'm feeling okay. But what if I have a relapse? It could happen anytime, and it could be serious. It could affect my heart, my lungs, my kidneys. I might have to go back in the hospital for a long time. There's no way of knowing." Holly shook her head grimly. "It's not romantic, Chris. I know. I've been through it already."

"If it happens, we'll deal with it," Chris promised. "That's what love is all about, right? Sticking with someone through thick and thin? Handling problems together?"

Holly nodded.

"And you're only looking on the dark side," Chris continued. "I went to the library yesterday and read a lot about lupus. The book said lupus is hardly ever a fatal disease. Eighty to ninety percent of people with lupus live at least ten years after they've been diagnosed. And there's all kinds of medications they can give you to control the symptoms."

Holly was impressed. The fact that Chris had gone to so much trouble to understand her illness proved, perhaps more than anything he'd said, that he was serious about her and willing to stand by her.

"Besides," Chris said with a grin, "I won't let you die. I love you too much. So what do you

say, Holly? Will you come away with me? Can
we think about the *beginning* of our life together, not the end?" He looked down at her
so tenderly, so lovingly, that there was only one
thing Holly could say.

"Okay," she whispered. "You win. When do
we leave?"

Chris lifted her up off the dance floor and
pressed his lips against hers. Holly kissed him
back passionately, aware that the tuxedos and
black dresses were all staring at them curiously,
and not caring at all.

"Hi, Elaine," June said, putting down her
hors d'oeuvre tray and coming around the
table to stand next to her friend.

Elaine, who was whispering something to
Brett, didn't seem to notice her.

"And, Brett! What a surprise!" June exclaimed, positioning herself behind the punch
bowl.

Brett tore his eyes away from Elaine and
glanced at her. For a second, he looked embarrassed. Then he gave June a charming smile.
"June," he said. "I've been meaning to call you."

Now Elaine looked at June, her curiosity
mixed with a little jealousy.

"No problem," June said brightly. She took the silver ladle out of the punch bowl and laid it on the white linen tablecloth, staining it bright red.

"Hey," Elaine said. "What are you doing?"

"I thought you could use some help," June said, smiling at Elaine. "Brett looks like he wants some punch."

Elaine picked up the ladle. "It's okay," she said. "I can serve him."

"You've been working too hard, Elaine," June insisted. "You've got to let me help you. Brett, you don't mind if I give you punch, do you?"

Brett shrugged. "I don't care."

"Good!" June said, lifting up the heavy bowl. The clear red fluid, with soggy slices of lemon floating in it, sloshed against the sides. A little spilled over the edge, splashing June's blouse.

"Hey!" Elaine exclaimed again. "What are you doing?"

Without another word, June heaved the bowl at Brett. The red juice hit him with full force. It soaked his face, his tuxedo, and dripped over his shiny black shoes, making a rapidly growing puddle on the floor. He stared at June, too stunned to move.

"Too bad this wasn't full of boiling water," June said, putting down the bowl with satisfaction. "You would have gotten burned the same way you like to burn others, you jerk!"

The bandleader tapped his baton on the podium, then all at once the trumpets started blasting the energetic intro to "Boogie Woogie Bugle Boy." All around Holly and Chris, couples broke apart and began to jitterbug to the swing rhythm.

"You want to?" Chris asked, stepping back from Holly and holding out his right hand. "I learned all the steps in ballroom dancing class when I was ten. I think I still remember 'em."

The lively beat was infectious, and Holly would have liked to twist and twirl the way everyone else was. But her feet were really sore now, and she felt so tired. "Would it be okay if we took a little rest?" she asked.

"Of course!" Chris led her toward a row of upholstered chairs that had been lined up along one side of the dance floor. "Sit down! Would you like something to eat or drink?"

"Sure," Holly said as she sat down.

"What would you like?" Chris asked. "There's a big buffet table over there with lobster, shrimp, caviar, pâté—"

"Aaaah!" Holly screamed. She'd been listening to Chris when she happened to look down at her aching feet, and the sight had been so hideous she hadn't been able to stop herself from crying out.

"What's the matter?" Chris asked, sitting down beside her.

Holly just pointed. When Chris looked down, his eyes widened in panic. Holly's legs and ankles had swollen to twice their normal size. They looked like giant water balloons, or watermelons, not anything remotely human. Holly's face was hot, too, and all her joints were aching. Holly raised a hand to her forehead. It was like touching a furnace.

Chris, too, touched Holly's face. "You're burning up," he said. "We've got to get you to the hospital right away. I'll be right back." He hopped up from his chair and dashed away through the dancing crowd.

"You're fired!" the maître d' screamed at June, his face red with fury. "Assaulting a guest! Disrupting a hotel function! You'll be lucky if we don't bring criminal charges!"

Brett, still sopping wet, was being patted down with linen napkins by his girlfriend.

Elaine stood nearby, looking confused. A bus-boy mopped the puddle of punch on the floor.

June, still standing behind the table, shrugged at the maître d' and smiled. "Sorry," she said. "I guess I must have slipped."

The maître d' turned worriedly to Brett. "Are you all right, sir?" he asked solicitously. "Don't worry. We'll take care of this." Then he turned back to June. "I want you out of here *now*! And don't ever show your face around this hotel again, do you understand?"

"Fine," June said. "I don't care if I never come back. Your guests are a bunch of hypo-critical snobs, and the people who work here aren't much better!" Grabbing a handful of shrimp balls, June popped one in her mouth.

"Those are for the guests!" the maître d' shouted, but June ignored him as she walked away. Nothing she'd ever eaten in her life had tasted so delicious.

As June made her way across the dance floor, she noticed Holly lying across three chairs while Chris knelt by her side looking crazed with fear. A small group of people stood around looking on and chattering nervously.

"Holly!" June shouted, pushing through the crowd of onlookers.

Holly's eyes were closed and her face was flushed. She moaned softly without opening her eyes.

June dropped to her knees next to Chris. "I'm Holly's sister June," she explained quickly. "What happened?"

"I'm not sure exactly," Chris said, "but the ambulance is on its way. Could you watch her while I run to the front? I want to show the medics the fastest way in."

June nodded. Chris jumped to his feet and ran off. June took Holly's feverish hand and held it against her face. "Can you hear me, Hol?" she asked. "It's June."

Holly nodded and moaned again.

"You're going to be okay," June promised. "The medics will be here any minute." Tears were running down June's cheeks, but she was determined not to let her fear show in her voice. The last thing she wanted was for Holly to be any more upset about her condition than she already was. "You're going to be okay," June repeated fiercely, convinced that if she just wished for it hard enough, she could make it come true.

Chapter Eighteen

"What's taking them so long!" Chris muttered impatiently as he paced back and forth across the pale gray linoleum floor. "She's been in there over an hour." Chris's tuxedo jacket was thrown carelessly on a blue molded plastic chair. His bow tie dangled out of his pants pocket, and he'd unbuttoned the top few buttons of his damp white shirt.

June knew she didn't look much better. She had splatters of fruit punch on the front of her white blouse, and she was sweating so much even her hair was wet. It was stifling here in the hospital waiting room. The air conditioner was broken and no breeze came in through the open windows.

"They're probably still running tests," June

informed him. "This is what happened last year when she collapsed."

"But she ended up being fine, right?" Chris said, coming to sit next to June on the fake leather couch.

"It was different last time," June said. "She was tired and achy, but her legs didn't swell up like that. This must be a new symptom."

"What does the swelling mean?"

June shrugged. "We've got so many brochures at home describing so many symptoms, I don't remember. But I know it's not good."

The swinging door opened and June's parents rushed in, their faces frantic. "June!" her mother exclaimed, opening her arms wide. June ran to her mother and hugged her, then her dad.

"Any news?" her father asked. June noticed he was wearing a pajama top with his jeans.

"Nothing since I called you," June said. "Dr. Frazier's still running some tests."

"This is my fault," Mrs. Paige said, sinking onto one of the plastic chairs. "I never should have let her work at the diner. It was too much for her. That's why she had a relapse."

Mr. Paige took a seat beside her and put his arm around her. "Don't blame yourself,

Peg. Anything could have triggered it."

Mrs. Paige wiped her red, swollen eyes with a crumpled tissue. "I just want to see her and tell her I love her," she said.

"Me, too," Chris said quietly to June.

June's mother finally noticed Chris and scowled. "What are *you* doing here?" she demanded.

June's father, too, looked up at Chris. "Is that who I think it is?" he asked.

June could smell trouble coming. She had to do everything in her power to prevent it. "Chris is the one who called the ambulance," she piped up. "He's been a big help."

"I'll bet," Mr. Paige said sarcastically.

Mrs. Paige was still staring angrily at Chris. "Was Holly with *you* tonight? She told us she was going to a friend's birthday party."

"*I'm* the friend," Chris said.

Mr. Paige then looked at June. "Wait a minute—the party you were working tonight at The Mountain. Was that the same party?"

June nodded mutely.

"Oh, I get it now," her father said, rising to his feet. "I should have realized that where there's trouble, a Franklin can't be far behind." He crossed the linoleum and stood over Chris.

"What did you do to her?" he asked accusingly.

Chris rose to his feet and calmly stared Mr. Paige in the eye. "Nothing," he said, "except ask her to be my date."

"I'm sure you'd like me to believe that!" Mr. Paige sniped. "Haven't you Franklins done enough to destroy my home and my family without resorting to this?"

The swinging doors opened and Chris's father strode into the room. "I heard that, Paige," he bellowed, putting a protective arm around Chris. "How dare you talk to my son that way!"

"It's okay, Dad," Chris said. "He's just upset about Holly. He doesn't know what he's saying."

"I know *exactly* what I'm saying," Mr. Paige snapped. "If I'd known Holly had anything to do with you, I would have locked her in her room!"

Mr. Franklin burst into loud, unpleasant laughter. "*You'd* forbid your daughter to see *my son*? I think you've got it backward. Your daughter's lucky a Franklin would have anything to do with her."

"Dad," Chris pleaded, placing a hand on his father's arm. He turned to Mr. Paige. "That's not true," he insisted.

But Mr. Paige wasn't listening. His face was

beet red and blue veins were bulging on his forehead. "How dare you!" he shouted up at Mr. Franklin. "How dare you lord your money and power and connections over my daughter! But you've been doing that to the whole town for ten years, so I guess I shouldn't be surprised. Well, everyone else may be afraid of you, Franklin, but I'm not! We can step outside and settle this right now, if you're man enough."

"You dare to threaten me!" Mr. Franklin shouted back. "A little nothing nobody like you? You're not even good enough to shine my shoes."

"SHUT UP!" Chris screamed at the top of his lungs, stepping between his father and June's. Both men were so surprised by his outburst that they fell silent. "What's the matter with you?" Chris shouted at them. "Why are you still fighting over something that happened ten years ago? Why aren't you thinking about what's happening *right now*? Holly's sick and we want her to get better. That's the only thing that matters."

"You have nothing to do with Holly," Mrs. Paige said, rising and joining her husband. "This is *our* family's problem. Not yours."

"It *is* my problem," Chris insisted. "I love

Holly. And Holly loves me. And neither one of us cares how any of you feel about that. We love each other, we're going to be together, and none of you can stop us!"

Mr. Franklin and the Paiges just stared at Chris, too shocked to say anything.

"How're you feeling?" Dr. Frazier asked Holly the next morning as he walked into her hospital room. Not very tall, and slight of build, he had dark brown skin and a close-cropped black Afro.

"Better, thanks," Holly said, boosting herself up to a sitting position. She wiggled her legs, which were now almost back to their normal size. "See!" she said. "The swelling's down. And the nurse just took my temperature. Just a little above normal."

"That's good, Holly," Dr. Frazier said. He pulled up a chair next to her bed and sat down. His face had a somber, serious expression. Holly looked at him nervously. Was he about to give her more bad news? She hadn't heard the results of any of the tests they'd given her. On the other hand, Dr. Frazier always looked serious, even when he was giving good news.

"So?" Holly asked. "Did you figure out what's wrong?"

Dr. Frazier nodded. "You've developed nephritis," he said. "In layman's terms—kidney disease."

Holly gasped. In all the brochures she'd read, kidney disease was always listed as the most serious complication of lupus, the one that could kill you.

"But . . ." Dr. Frazier said, holding up his hand, "before you get too worried, here's the good news. You have a very mild case. We did a biopsy last night and found almost no inflammation or scarring. You did have high levels of protein in your urine, however. That's what made you retain all that fluid."

"Is there anything you can do about it?" Holly asked, only somewhat comforted by the "good news." "I mean, it could happen again or get worse, right?"

"It could," Dr. Frazier admitted, "but we can control your condition with some simple measures that should make that unlikely."

"Simple measures?" Holly asked.

Dr. Frazier nodded. "We're putting you on a brief course of Prednisone—that's a kind of steroid drug—which should reverse the nephritis. And for a few more days we'll be giving you diuretics to drain the extra fluid. Then, when your blood and urine levels are normal, you can go home."

Holly was surprised and relieved. "And that's it?"

"Well, of course we'll want to monitor you," Dr. Frazier said. "And you'll have to watch your salt and protein intake. But there's every reason to be optimistic. With the proper treatment, the risk of complete kidney failure is only about ten percent. And even then, there are things we can do to treat it."

Holly sighed. While she knew she should be happy her condition wasn't even more serious, all she could think about was the fact that she was back in the hospital again. Even if she did go home, and even if she did feel fine, she could never escape this illness as long as she lived. And now she had kidney failure to worry about, too. Even if the odds were low, they were still there.

Dr. Frazier rose and put a comforting hand on Holly's shoulder. "Don't worry, Holly," he said. "We're going to take care of you. You're going to be all right."

Holly nodded, trying to look convinced.

*   *   *

"You want to do *what?*" Chris's father raged, slamming his fist against the antique formal dining-room table. "Are you out of your mind?"

"Bill," Chris's mother said, "be careful. This table's two hundred years old."

Bill Franklin turned his fury on his wife. "Our son is throwing away his future and all you can worry about is your stupid table?"

"Don't talk to Mom like that," Chris defended her.

His father turned back to Chris, his eyes cold and glittering. "This isn't about the dining-room table. It's about *you, your life.* How could you even *consider* giving up Yale for this girl? How can you be so shortsighted?"

"I already told you, Dad," Chris said. "I love her."

Mr. Franklin sneered. "It's not love. How can it be? You barely know her. It's just youthful infatuation."

"Don't tell me how I feel!" Chris yelled. "You don't know a thing about it."

"Here's what I know," Mr. Franklin said, pushing back his antique chair and standing up. "If you go through with this ridiculous idea, you'll never get another cent from me."

"Oh, big surprise," Chris said mockingly. "I

expected you'd cut me off, just like you did to Blaire. You think your money gives you some kind of power over us? Do you think either one of us cares? She doesn't need your money, and neither do I!"

Miranda, the maid, came in to clear the table, but Chris's mother waved her back to the kitchen. "Please, Bill," she begged. "Does it have to come to this again? We've already lost one child."

"We didn't lose her," Mr. Franklin said. "Blaire chose her fate. I'm trying to *stop* Chris from making the same mistake." His big, rugged face softened, became sad. "Chris," he said. "I'm begging you. Listen to me. We're just trying to prevent you from making a mistake you'll regret for the rest of your life. We just want what's best for you."

"That's exactly what I'm talking about!" Chris shouted, also standing. "It's always been about what *you* want for me. Never what I want."

"You think I've worked this hard for *me*?" his father demanded. "Who do you think is going to get everything after I'm gone? Everything I've ever done I've done for my children."

"That's a crock, and you know it," Chris exclaimed. "You just said you'd cut me off unless I did what you wanted, and you already did it to Blaire. You think you can program us to follow your instructions. Well, it doesn't work that way, Dad. Blaire has the right to live her own life, and so do I."

Chris's father just glared. In the dim light of the dining room, the candelabra on the formally set table cast weird flickering shadows on his face.

"Don't you see?" Chris went on. "By pushing us so hard, you ended up pushing us away. That's why Blaire ran off. Since you wouldn't give her any freedom, she had to find it herself. She got away just in time, too. Before you slipped that noose around her neck. And that's what I've got to do, too. That's why I'm leaving. I've got to figure out who I really am before you take it away from me."

Mr. Franklin sank slowly into his seat. He looked thoughtful. Chris wondered if maybe his father had heard what he'd said, was starting to understand. Finally, his father spoke. "Don't do it, Chris," he warned. "If you disobey me and leave with that girl, I promise you, you'll be very, very sorry."

Chapter Nineteen

A huge bouquet of colorful flowers were being delivered to Holly's hospital room. Holly couldn't see who was holding the flowers, only that the person wore a pair of blue jeans.

"Hello?" Holly asked curiously.

The flowers were set down on Holly's bed tray, and Chris's face appeared above them. "What?" he asked, grinning broadly. "Didn't you recognize me?"

"Sorry," Holly said with a smile. "I had you confused with a bunch of petunias."

Chris leaned over Holly and gave her a long, firm kiss on the lips. "You look a lot better than you did last night!" he said when they finally broke apart. He sat down in the chair beside her bed and took hold of Holly's hand.

"I feel better just seeing you," Holly confessed, bringing his hand to her cheek. "They should bottle you and give you to me as medicine."

"That would be fine with me," Chris said, sliding the chair closer.

"See," Holly said grimly. "I told you loving me wasn't going to be easy. If you want to back out now, I totally understand."

Chris just squeezed her hand tighter. "Nothing's changed!" he insisted. "Don't you understand that? I said I'd stand by you no matter what. And we've got traveling plans. You think I want to miss out on that?"

Chris reached into the bouquet of flowers and pulled out a small plastic model of a red Jeep. It looked exactly like Chris's.

"Here," Chris said, handing the model to Holly.

"What's this for?" Holly asked, spinning the rubber wheels with her finger.

"Just a reminder of what you have to look forward to when you get out of here."

Holly sighed. "Oh Chris," she said. "It's sweet that you still want to go, but how can we? Dr. Frazier wants to keep an eye on me, so I can't go far. And what if I have another relapse? It would just be too complicated."

"I've already talked to Dr. Frazier," Chris said, "and he said there's no reason why you can't travel. You just have to make sure to take your medication and check in with a doctor on a regular basis. He could even give you a copy of your medical records to take with you."

Holly tried to imagine herself in a red Jeep on the open road, popping Prednisone and diuretics. Not exactly the travel fantasy she'd had all her life. Then she imagined Chris having to pull over on the side of the road as she slumped in the front seat, doubled over in pain. An ambulance wailed in the distance, red lights flashing, then pulled up alongside the Jeep. The next thing Holly saw was herself right back here in this hospital bed.

No, now that her condition had worsened, her travel fantasy could only be that. A *fantasy*. Holly had to make Chris realize this somehow.

"We *can't* go," Holly insisted. "It's not that I don't want to. I do, more than I've ever wanted anything."

"So what's stopping us?" Chris asked, his face full of cheerful optimism.

Holly felt tears rise to her eyes, and her throat felt thick and tight. But she wasn't going to let Chris see her cry. It was easy for him to ignore the hard facts. *He* wasn't the one who was sick—possibly dying. What did he understand about not getting what you wanted? All his life, his parents had given him everything. And he had years and years ahead of him, years of good health and unlimited money and anything else he wanted.

"You just don't get it, do you?" Holly snapped. "You're just like your father."

Chris's face darkened. "What's that supposed to mean?"

"You think you can just snap your fingers and get your way. You think the whole world will go along with your plan just because you're a Franklin."

Chris looked so hurt, so surprised, that Holly wanted to throw her arms around him and apologize immediately. But she was on a roll now. She couldn't stop herself.

"Well, it doesn't work that way," Holly continued. "I'm *sick*. And not even your money can change that."

Now Chris's eyes filled with tears. "I never said that!" he insisted. "I never even thought it!"

Holly couldn't stand to see how unhappy she was making him, but it was the only way. "It just won't work. I can't kid myself. My life is coming to an end a lot sooner that yours," she insisted. "So you might as well go home. It was nice knowing you."

"Holly . . ."

Holly rolled over in bed so her back was to him. She felt Chris's hand rest on her shoulder, soft, warm, and comforting. Shrugging it away, Holly pulled the blanket up. "Good-bye, Chris," she said. Her body, her face, even her voice was rigid. She wasn't going to let herself cry, even now.

"Holly . . ." Chris pleaded. "Please look at me."

"*Good-bye.*" Holly squeezed her eyes shut and pulled the blanket up over her ears. She could sense Chris still standing there, hoping she'd turn around and say something. But Holly couldn't give in. This was the way it had to be. The sooner they both faced it, the easier it would be in the long run.

After a few minutes, Chris silently left the room. As soon as she heard the door close quietly behind him, Holly burst into tears.

"But why won't you let me help, Mom?" Holly asked her frazzled mother, who stood at the grill cooking three orders of scrambled eggs, two omelettes, flapjacks, home fries, and a dozen breakfast sausages. "Rita didn't show up today, and Liz can't take care of all the orders by herself."

Peg Paige wiped some stray strands of hair out of her face with her forearm. "No, Holly. You've only been out of the hospital a couple days. You need your rest."

"But I feel fine!" Holly insisted. "Better than I did before I went into the hospital." Noticing the omelettes looked ready, Holly grabbed two heavy white plates and held them out for her mother to put them on.

Her mother grabbed the plates and put them down on the counter. "For the last time, *no*. Dr. Frazier said you were probably overexerting yourself. That's why you got sick again."

"He didn't say that was definitely what caused it," Holly argued. "He said it *might* have been the reason."

Peg Paige slipped her spatula under the omelettes and shoveled them onto the plates. "If there's even a chance that's what caused it, then that's enough for me," she said. "From now on, miss, you're a lady of leisure." Using her spatula again, she scooped up some home fries and sausages and dumped them next to each omelette.

"But I'm *bored*," Holly complained as her mother carried the omelette plates to the kitchen window and rang the bell. "Maybe I'll go for a walk."

"No, Holly," her mother said. "Just relax. Or study for your high-school equivalency. That's not strenuous."

Holly sighed and left the kitchen. Her parents were just as much like prison guards as Chris's. *Chris*. Why was she even *thinking* about him? Chris was history as far as Holly was concerned. She hadn't seen him since that day in the hospital, over a week ago. Chris must have gotten her message loud and clear.

By now, Holly was sure, he'd moved on, found someone else. Some cute, rich blond girl in a short skirt he'd met on the tennis court. Someone his parents approved of. Someone who might live to see her eighteenth birthday.

Not that Holly blamed Chris. She'd pushed him away. What choice did he have but to go on with his life? Just as Holly had to go on with hers, what was left of it, anyway. Her short insignificant life in tiny Landon. Well, the one good thing about being stuck here was that time would go so slowly her life would *feel* longer.

Pushing through the kitchen door, Holly went back to the booth by the window where she'd spent the morning. Her trigonometry textbook was still open to the chapter on sines, cosines, and tangents. Holly liked math, especially algebra and trig, but she could only focus on it for so long. Holly sank down onto the red vinyl seat patched with black electric tape. Maybe she should switch to another subject. She'd brought her world history textbook.

The front door opened and Annie and Sal entered with glum faces. Seeing Holly, they shuffled over.

"What's the matter, guys?" Holly asked, sliding farther into the booth so her sisters could join her.

"They announced the winner of the New England Mountain Bike contest," Sal said, pouting.

"And it wasn't us," Annie added, sinking down in her seat so she could put her feet up on the seat opposite.

"It's so unfair," Sal complained. "We really needed those bikes, too."

Holly hugged her sisters comfortingly. "That stinks," she said. "Who won?"

The front door opened again, and Jay

Lawrence lumbered in wearing baggy overalls, a wrinkled T-shirt, and heavy tan work boots. Right behind him, dressed identically, was Cynthia Dansby! Her hair hung lank and straight. Not only did she wear no makeup, but she actually had a streak of bicycle grease on her cheek.

"No," Holly said in horror, glancing at her sisters. "Not her!"

The twins nodded.

"I can't believe Jay fell for it!" Holly exclaimed. "Cynthia? The Spirit of the Mountains?"

"I bet she won't even ride her new bike," Sal said. "All she cares about is modeling in the advertisement."

Annie, who was at the far end of the seat, jumped up. "But we've got a new plan for getting us some bikes," she said. "*The Landon Observer* is looking for kids to deliver the paper. If we save up our money, we should be able to get 'em by the end of September."

Sal jumped up, too. "We're heading over there now. We just stopped by for some doughnuts."

Annie and Sal ran behind the counter, where they each took a sugary jelly doughnut from the glass case.

"See ya!" they shouted as they ran outside.

Holly smiled as she watched them jump on their worn-out bikes. That's what she loved about *all* her sisters. They never let anything get them down for long. June already had her eye on some new guy she'd met at her new job serving ice cream at Harry's Homemade Ice Cream Parlor. Holly wished she could bounce back so easily, but it was hard to feel optimistic when she had nothing to look forward to.

Holly heard the distant roar of a powerful engine, then saw a red Jeep pull up in front of the diner. Chris jumped out of the driver's seat and walked briskly to the front door. His face looked grim and determined.

Holly grew tense. What had he come to tell her? Maybe he wanted to rub his newfound happiness in Holly's face. Holly looked back at the Jeep, expecting to see his blond, tennis-playing girlfriend in the front seat, but there was no one there.

Chris came through the front door and looked around the diner. Spotting Holly, he approached her without any change in expression. "Come on," he said in a hushed voice. "It's time to go."

"Go where?" Holly asked.

Chris reached into the back pocket of his

chinos and pulled out a long, narrow piece of paper. "See this?" he asked, waving the paper in her face. "It's a check for five thousand dollars. Every cent of it's my own money. Not a penny of it comes from my father."

Holly looked at Chris blankly. What was he getting at?

"This should be enough to get started," Chris said. "If we need more, we'll figure out a way to earn more." He grabbed Holly's hand and tried to pull her up out of her seat.

"Wait a minute! Slow down, Chris," Holly said. "I don't understand."

"We're leaving," Chris said. "On that trip we talked about. You didn't think I forgot, did you?"

Holly stared at Chris, her mouth agape. "But how can we go now? I told you I was sick. And we're not seeing each other anymore. . . ."

"I'm seeing you right now," Chris said. "And I'm planning to see a lot more of you if you'll just get in the car with me."

Holly couldn't believe Chris was even talking to her after all the horrible things she'd said to him. "Why are you doing this?" she asked.

"Because I love you," Chris said fiercely,

"and I always will. And however long you have—a week, a month, a year, or a lifetime—I want to be with you."

Holly felt her eyes grow hot with tears. "You still feel that way about me?" she whispered. "Even now?"

"I'll *always* feel this way," Chris said. "And I'll always want to give you everything. Like this trip. We can still do it. If you get sick again, we can always turn back. Don't deny yourself happiness, Holly. And don't deny me the chance to be with you."

Holly was gripping the table so hard her knuckles were white, but she was afraid to let go. If she did, she was afraid she'd follow Chris right out the door.

Chris gently covered one of Holly's hands with his own and lifted it easily from the table. "Come on," he encouraged her. "Let's leave this place."

Holly's resistance was weakening, but she couldn't give in. "What about your parents?" she asked. "How are they going to feel that you're giving up Yale and law school and your big future in Washington?"

"Let *me* worry about that," Chris said. "I'm not afraid of them anymore. The only thing I'm afraid of is not being with you."

Holly still had one more argument to make. "We haven't told anybody we're leaving," he said. "I haven't even packed a suitcase."

Chris pointed to his car. "It's in the backseat."

"What is?"

"Your suitcase. I talked to June this morning and she packed it for you, including all your medications and prescriptions. My stuff's in there, too. So what are you waiting for?"

"But my parents . . ." Holly began.

"Don't tell them," Chris warned. "If you do, we'll never get out of this town."

Holly knew Chris was right. Still, how could she just up and leave without saying good-bye? "But my parents will be so worried about me," she argued.

"We'll call them as soon as we're a safe distance away." Chris sat beside Holly and clasped her hand in both of his. "The moment is now, Holly," he said. "If you don't jump on this opportunity, it's going to pass away forever."

Holly's heart began to pound. Could she actually do this? All she had to do was get up from her seat, walk a few yards across the diner, open the door, and jump in the car. It would only take a few seconds. It should be easy. But doing it felt as scary as jumping off a cliff.

Still holding on to Holly's hand, Chris stood up. "C'mon, Holly," he said. "I know it's scary, but I'll be with you every step of the way. Together, we can do it."

Holly glanced toward the kitchen window. She could just see the back of her mother's head at the grill. Any second now, her mother could turn around and the moment would be lost. Closing her eyes, Holly took a deep breath. Then she jumped up out of her seat. "Let's go now," she whispered to Chris. "Before I come to my senses."

"Whoa!" Holly shouted into the wind as it streamed over her face and whipped at her hair. With one hand, she held on to her straw hat so it wouldn't blow off down the long stretch of highway that already lay between them and Landon, twenty miles behind. On either side of them, pine-covered mountains rose to distant peaks. Ahead of them, the road stretched endlessly into the distance. "I can't believe we really did it!" Holly shouted. "We're free!"

Chris grinned beneath his black Ray•Ban

sunglasses. His hair, too, streamed behind him in the onrush of wind. "Feels great, doesn't it?" he asked, turning to glance at Holly.

"It feels incredible!" Holly said, grinning back at him.

For a few moments they drove on, just enjoying the breeze and the mountains. Holly half expected to see the sheriff chasing after them with his siren wailing, but the road was as empty behind them as it was in front of them.

"So?" Holly asked after a few more minutes. "What's our plan?"

"We don't have to plan anything," Chris said, turning on the radio to a loud rock station. "From now on, we live one day at a time."

"Sounds good!" Holly said. "But where are we going?"

Chris pointed to the glove compartment. "Look in there," he said.

Holly opened the glove compartment and found a huge foldout map of the United States.

"You pick!" Chris shouted over the wind. "Anywhere you want. Just point to the place, and I'll take you there."

Holly felt giddy with love and freedom. Just a few moments ago, she'd felt like a prisoner.

Now the whole country was at her fingertips. Holly studied the map with its pastel states and spidery, squiggly network of highways. There were so many places she'd never been, so many places she wanted to go. It was hard to choose.

But there were two words in bold black type that caught her eye more than any others. A city she'd only seen in movies and on television, a city that seemed to be the center of everything exciting and glamorous and new.

"New York!" Holly announced, putting her finger on the map. "I've always wanted to go there. Let's make that our first stop."

"Your wish is my command!" Chris said, pressing his foot on the accelerator.

The Jeep took off, carrying with it all of Holly's hopes that a bright future with Chris was just beginning.

Join Holly and Chris on their romantic journey in Book II, Good-bye to Love.